Steam

Steam

A Lesbian Romance

Properties Of Love
Book 2

Tessa Vidal

Edited by
Beverly Hernandez

For my sister, Rita.

Prologue
Samantha- 22 Years Ago

"I'm only dating Billy because he's the most popular boy in school." I flipped my hair over my shoulder. "And you'd better not tell anyone I said that."

"I think he's dreamy," Tammy sighed dramatically, and it took all my self-control not to gag. "Plus he's rich. The Turner's own the largest pecan farm in south Georgia."

"Who cares?" I picked up the pace. Tammy was my next-door neighbor. Her parents owned the Teeterville Tire Company and were hardly poor. They were intent on marrying Tammy and her sister Julie off to boys who came from so-called good families. But the pickings were slim, considering the town had less than three thousand people.

"Do your folks like him?" Tammy's skinny legs raced to keep up with me. I hated this entire conversation and was hoping she'd get the hint. Billy Turner was just a way to pass the time until I could escape this boring little town. "My parents would love it if I could go out with a boy like Billy."

It tempted me to tell her she could have him, but I still had

1

two more years of high school. After that, I was moving to Atlanta. That's where my life would really begin.

"If I ever get bored with him, I'll send Billy your way." I mumbled. Berrien County High School came into view, thank God. At least Tammy would shut the hell up about my loser boyfriend Billy when we got there.

"You don't really like him, do you?" Tammy said from behind me. I stopped and turned around.

"I have dreams, and living in Teeterville isn't one of them." I shrugged. "C'mon, we're gonna be late for first period."

What I didn't say was that living in this hellhole would be even worse if I wasn't popular. Currently, I was class president, on the cheerleading squad, and I was in the drama club. Billy Turner was the star quarterback. The girls thought he was a catch, but he only seemed to have eyes for me. Dating him was only a way to pass the time until I could escape this small town hell.

The first day of school at Berrien County High was always hard. The walls were covered with cracked white paint, and the floors were a dull shade of gray. Everywhere I looked, there were reminders of my small town life. Even after three years, the same old fears never seemed to go away.

It seemed like nothing had changed since I was a freshman. The same annoying kids clogged up the hallways, gossiping about their summer vacations and upcoming classes. I'd grown accustomed to the stares—the way everyone instantly knew who I was—but it still made me uncomfortable. In some ways, it felt like the entire school revolved around me and my clique, but I wanted more than that from life.

I wanted money and glamor, and living in Teeterville wasn't helping matters.

"Who's that?" Tammy elbowed me after we'd opened our lockers. "We never get new students."

"Bless her heart, whoever she is, she's gonna hate it here." I slammed my locker shut and inspected the new girl. Jesus, she was a knockout. She was tall like me, thin, with alabaster skin and wavy auburn hair that hung to her waist. She had an air of sophistication around her—like she'd been born into money or something.

But then I noticed the AirPods in her ears, the designer backpack slung over one shoulder, and it all clicked. This girl was from a big city like Atlanta—and she wasn't about to stick around Teeterville for long. I felt a twinge of envy as I watched her make her way down the hall, completely unperturbed by the stares following her every move.

I wanted that freedom—the freedom of not caring what anyone else thought of me and just living life on my own terms. But here in Teeterville, it seemed like it would never happen. No matter how hard I tried, I couldn't seem to escape this tiny town without making someone unhappy—my parents included.

"She's beautiful." Tammy's cheeks turned pink, and not for the first time did I wonder if she felt about girls the same way I did. Not that I'd ever share that information with anyone. There might be gay people on television, but that didn't mean it was safe to be out of the closet here. I only knew of two gay people- Jimmy Fogle, the town florist, and Thomas Luke, who cut my hair. Neither of them seemed particularly happy, and both pretended to have girlfriends. But they'd been living together since I was a kid, and it was an open secret that they were boyfriends. There were probably others, but unless you were obvious about being queer, people assumed you were straight.

Personally, I wasn't sure what I was. All I knew was that I'd much rather hang out with the girls instead of giving Billy a handsy in the back of his pickup truck.

"Hurry up." Tammy grabbed my elbow and steered me into homeroom. The bell rang, and we hurried into our seats. The new girl's frame filled the doorway of the classroom, and she had a confused look on her face.

"Is this Mrs. Floyd's classroom?" She asked, and my ears pricked up. The new girl didn't have an accent like the rest of us. It was more polished and sophisticated.

"Yes." Mrs. Floyd stood up from her desk and gestured toward the sea of desks in front of her.

The new girl made her way to the back of the class, her steps echoing in the room. She didn't seem to notice the stares she was getting from all corners of the classroom; instead, she politely smiled and said hello to Mrs. Floyd as she took a seat next to me.

The new girl had the longest legs I'd ever seen, and it surprised me no one had called her out for the short skirt she was wearing. Where on earth did she get her clothes? She must have bought them in a big city because none of the shops in the town square sold anything as revealing her outfit.

"Ladies and gentlemen, I hope you had a wonderful summer." Mrs. Floyd beamed at us. "My peach cobbler won a blue ribbon at the county fair, as it has for the last four years. I want each of you to stand up, introduce yourself, and tell us one thing that made your summer break fun." The teacher glanced around before settling on the new girl. "You're new to Berrien High, and I want to officially welcome you. Please stand up and tell us your name and something you loved about summer vacation."

Since we were at the rear of the class, everyone turned in their seats to look at her. She rolled her eyes, and without thinking, I snickered. Then she got to her feet.

"My name is Morgan Popescu." She placed her hands on her hips and a slow smile spread across her cheeks. "I spent the summer in Bucharest visiting family, and then I moved here." The new girl yawned, stretching her arms over her head. She was obviously not impressed with what she saw.

"Bucharest." Mrs. Floyd murmured. "Class, who knows where Bucharest is?"

I knew the answer, but most of the other kids stared down at their desks.

"It's in Romania." Mrs. Floyd smiled. "What brings you to our charming little town, Morgan?"

"They stationed dad at Moody Air Force Base, so they forced me to move here." The girl sat down, probably hoping Mrs. Floyd would shut the hell up. The base was thirty minutes from here in Valdosta.

"While it's not as cosmopolitan here compared to Europe, Teeterville has its charms." Mrs. Floyd's southern accent thickened. "Samantha, stand up and tell us about your summer."

Reluctantly, I got to my feet. I glanced down at the new girl, and I'd swear she was trying not to laugh.

"My summer was an absolute delight," I said sarcastically as I scanned the room. "I stayed home with my parents and did the normal country stuff. You know—swimming in the lake, having bonfires, fishing."

"And screwing Billy Turner at Lake Lewis." A lone voice whispered. I scowled and sat down.

Mrs. Floyd smiled sweetly, oblivious to the asshole teasing me. "That sounds lovely, Samantha. How about you Tim?"

She forced each of us to stand up and talk about our boring summers. The new girl was lucky. I'd take a European summer any day over mine. I glanced over at Morgan and was shocked to see her eyes trained on me. She nodded toward Mrs. Floyd, then rolled her eyes dramatically. That seemed to be her go to expression, rolling her eyes.

"The bell's about to ring." Mrs. Floyd sat down behind her scratched wooden desk. "Samantha, please be Morgan's guide today. Show her around the school and introduce her to all of your friends." The bell rang, and everyone leapt to their feet.

"Are all the teachers as dorky as her?" Morgan whispered.

"Unfortunately, yes."

* * *

"Hey babe," Billy's arm circled my waist. Morgan smirked as he planted a kiss on my cheek. Billy turned to her and grinned. "Who are you?"

"This is Morgan." I nodded in her direction. Normally, I tolerated Billy, but for some reason, I couldn't stand him touching me. I shrugged off his arm. "We'd stay and talk, but we have to go to gym class."

He placed his arms on my shoulders and tried to kiss me on the lips.

"Not now, Billy." I frowned. "C'mon, Morgan. It's time for fifty minutes of torture."

"What's the matter with you?" Billy scowled, and I walked away without answering. Morgan followed along, then she stopped and whispered in my ear.

"Let me guess. That guy is the king of the jocks, and you're a cheerleader." She winked at me, and I felt heat racing up my neck.

"Yes, and yes." I huffed and resumed walking. "Billy's alright. But as soon as I graduate, I'm getting out of this hellhole."

Morgan looped her arm through mine, something most girls didn't do around here. Maybe it was a European thing?

"By hellhole, do you mean this town, the school, or both?"

"Both." I giggled. "Billy's a good ole boy who will work for his dad after graduation. He's expecting me to spread my legs and pump out a few babies. But I have other plans."

"I thought you'd already done that." Morgan murmured.

"Done what?"

Morgan stopped walking so suddenly that I bounced against her. Her emerald green eyes were wide and bright, as if the sunlight bouncing off them made them shine.

"You know, fuck the hillbilly. He's not bad looking, if you're into guys."

"I didn't...I mean..." I stammered, but the words wouldn't come to me.

"You're not, are you? Into guys?" Morgan persisted. Jesus, she'd just met me, and it was like she could read my mind.

All the color drained from my face.

"No," I whispered. "Are you?"

Chapter One
Morgan

"Rob, is there anything else?" I closed my laptop and slid it into my leather briefcase. "The driver is about to pull into the hotel parking lot."

"Netflix is picking up the series, *Enigma de la Miezul Nopții*." Rob couldn't pronounce it right. In English it was *Midnight Enigma*. It was a Romanian detective series I'd worked on four years ago before hitting it big on Broadway. "You'll get a tidy sum from them within the next six months."

"And zero royalties forever after." I sighed. Streaming services were notorious for underpaying creatives like me. "Rob, let me call you back in a few hours. I want to get settled in first." The driver parked the car in front of the hotel, and the trunk popped open. I disconnected the call before my agent could say anything else. He was long-winded on a good day.

The driver opened the back door of the BMW and said, "Miss Sterling." I stepped out into the crisp Los Angeles air and grabbed my briefcase off the seat. Then I turned toward the hotel - an imposing structure standing tall against a backdrop of rolling hills. The Chateau Marmont, one of the most exclusive hotels in the world. Rob had paid them for three months in advance, all because of Lindsay Lohan. The hotel banned her from staying here years ago for not paying her bill, so now everyone paid upfront.

I walked up to the front desk and waited for someone to greet me. A few minutes later, a woman wearing a neatly pressed uniform approached me with a smile. "Welcome to Chateau Marmont! How may I help you today?"

I gave her my name, and she nodded in recognition before getting to work. She typed something into her computer and then handed me a key card, along with several forms. After I finished filling them out, she assigned a porter to me and wished me a pleasant stay.

Walking down the hallway to my room, I felt a sense of grandeur. The walls were covered in beautiful tapestries, and there were elegant velvet curtains hanging from tall windows that overlooked the hills outside.

"Let me open the door for you, Miss Sterling." The porter stepped in front of me for a moment and opened the door.

When I entered my suite, I gasped.

"Jesus."

I couldn't believe my eyes. The room was larger than any apartment I had ever lived in before. They filled every inch of the space with luxurious furniture and decor, from the plush carpets to the velvet drapes hanging from the tall windows.

"Put my bags in the bedroom, please," I said to the older man with a smile.

I walked around my temporary home, taking in every detail. The living area was appointed with two cozy armchairs facing a large flat screen TV mounted on one wall. An elegant writing desk sat under one of the windows, next to shelves filled with books - an invitation to unwind after a long day on set.

The kitchen had high-quality appliances and cooking tools, which were perfect for me because I loved being in the kitchen.

"Will there be anything else, Miss Sterling?" The porter called from the living room. I strolled over to him and placed a twenty-dollar bill in his hand.

"That will be all." I stepped back and gestured toward the door. "Thanks for your help."

When he was gone, I went into the bedroom. Of course, it was stunning. In the center of it stood an enormous four-poster bed with a lavish comforter and matching pillows. There was also a balcony outside the bedroom. The doors were open, and a cool breeze filled the room with the scent of flowers and car exhaust.

"You've outdone yourself, Rob."

I pushed one of my suitcases to the side and laid next to it on the bed. Despite the luxurious suite, I was dying to get a place of my own. I had spent most of my career living in hotel rooms, and I truly wanted to have a place to call home.

After graduating from Julliard in New York, I'd gotten most of my acting jobs in Europe. Minor roles at first, then I scored a highly coveted role at London's Savoy Theatre in Noel Coward's *Private Lives*. After that, I got a role every actor dreams about in New York.

Echoes Of Elysium changed my life. The play tells the story of two star-crossed lovers, Elizabeth and William, whose paths first cross on a picturesque boardwalk. Elizabeth is a free-spirited local artist, and William is a wealthy businessman from the city, escaping to a coastal town for a much-needed break.

Their initial encounter leads to a whirlwind summer romance that audiences loved. Now, I was starring in the film adaption, my first major Hollywood movie.

"It's hard to believe I used to live in that tacky small town," I chuckled. Teeterville, Georgia, had been a miserable place. The only good thing that happened there was falling for Samantha. But after she disappeared, I'd quickly moved on to school in New York. I often wondered how she was doing. Did she end up marrying what's his name? Or did she escape like I did?

"Whatever," I sighed, then I heard my phone ringing from the other room. I forced myself off the bed and raced into the living room.

"Miss Sterling?" A woman's voice sang through the phone.

"Yes?"

"This is Eva Thorne." The woman had a slightly nasal accent. "I want to welcome you to Hollywood personally. Things are a little different here compared to New York."

Eva was the director of the movie and was very well respected in the industry. When I first met her, I'd immediately been drawn to her vision of the film.

"Eva, yes, thank you for calling." I noticed a bar next to the bookshelf and crossed the room to pour myself a drink. "Have you spoken to my agent Rob yet about rehearsals?"

"I just got off the phone with him, which reminds me. He wants you to call him as soon as possible." I heard ice tinkling in a glass and realized I wasn't the only one enjoying an afternoon cocktail. "He mentioned something about a realtor."

"Oh, thank God." I smiled. "The Chateau Marmont is lovely, but I'm looking for something more permanent."

"If the movie performs as expected, you'll be flooded with offers." Eva said, and I poured a shot of tequila. "Enough to keep you busy for years. Anyhow, we're doing a read through with the entire cast the day after tomorrow at Paramount."

"What time?"

"We'll start at ten, break for lunch at twelve, and we should be done by three. After that, I'll meet with you and Billy alone to give you notes." Eva referred to my co-star on stage and now the movie version of Echoes, Billy Grant. He was an amazing actor, but he tended to hit the bottle a little too much for my liking. Billy was one of the few actors on Broadway who didn't mind taking time off so his understudy could take the stage. Usually, it was because he had a hangover.

"Thanks for letting me know. Is there anything else?"

"You're more than welcome." I could hear the smile in Eva's voice. "I just wanted to say hello and welcome you to Hollywood personally. You've got what it takes to make it here." She paused for a long moment. "I'll see you at Paramount the day after tomorrow."

After disconnecting the call, I wandered through the suite. Though it was one of the nicest hotels I'd ever stayed at, it still felt off somehow.

"Damn it, I want an actual home." I flopped on the couch and stared up at the ceiling. When I first started acting in New York, it was exhilarating. But after years of hopping from one hotel to another, it had become exhausting. I longed for a place to call my own.

I grabbed my phone and searched for homes for sale in

Hollywood and instantly felt overwhelmed. "How the hell do people afford to live here?"

I was being paid handsomely for Echoes, but these prices were ludicrous. "Jesus," I muttered as I read over a listing for a three-bedroom home in Laurel Canyon. Three and a half million dollars for a house that would probably sell for a tenth of that price back in South Georgia. But this was where the action was, so if I wanted a permanent home in Los Angeles, I was going to pay through the nose for it.

A text message flashed across the screen from my agent, Ron.

Call me ASAP

I pressed the little phone icon next to his message, and a moment later, he answered.

"Hey love, I've got a list of real estate agencies for you. I'll email you them to you right now." He was breathing heavily, and I wondered if he'd started smoking again. "Nathan Lane highly recommends Iconic California Estates. I'm setting up an appointment for myself. Do you want me to set one up for you, too?"

"I didn't know you were moving from New York." I frowned. Ron was the best in the business, but he could be overbearing. Hopefully, he wouldn't want us living next door to each other.

"Now that you're signed to Paramount, most of my clients are here. Gotta be where the money is, you know what I mean?" Ron coughed.

"Okay, but they sound very expensive." I shut my eyes for a moment and imagined myself living in a sprawling mansion overlooking the ocean. "They deal with estates, and all I want is a pleasant little house. You know, just two or three bedrooms and a fancy kitchen."

"I'm sure they have something in your price range." He coughed again, and I shook my head. Damn idiot would kill himself if he didn't quit the cancer sticks.

"Set up an appointment with them for me." I yawned. "Oh, and not for the day after tomorrow. I've got a read through at the studio."

"Duh," Ron laughed. "I'm the one who controls your calender. As soon as I set up an appointment with ICE, I'll text you."

"Thanks, Ron." I disconnected the call.

My mind buzzed with the promise of a new chapter in Hollywood. With the success of Echoes, my career was on the brink of a breakthrough. Yet, amid the grandeur of the hotel and the prospect of a Hollywood home, a subtle longing tugged at my heart.

I couldn't help but wonder, would my journey to stardom in Hollywood fulfill more than just my career ambitions? Would I find a place to truly call home?

Chapter Two
Samantha

My head felt like I split it in two, and I couldn't remember the last time I'd felt this bad. Actually, yesterday morning sucked too. I rolled over and felt the warmth of someone next to me. Startled, I woke up with a start and my body tensed as I tried to recall what had happened the night before. Who the hell is in my bed?

An arm lay over my stomach, and the unfamiliar sound of a soft snore purred in my ear. I opened my eyes, and saw tousled red hair, freckled skin, and detected the faint smell of sex in the air. I had no memory of bringing anyone home with me last night, yet here she was sleeping soundly, her chest moving up and down with each breath.

My mind raced as I puzzled over how I had ended up here. I certainly hadn't planned on anything like this, and yet here I was in bed with a stranger. Was this a mistake? A drunken one-night stand? Whatever it was, I knew I had to get the stranger out of here and get ready for work.

Carefully, I slid out of bed and cautiously looked around the room, gathering my clothes as I went.

"Good morning, sexy lady."

I froze at the sound of the stranger's voice. Shit, what was her name?

"Last night was so good. I think it deserves an encore."

I slowly turned around, forcing a smile onto my face. "Good morning."

The woman, who was quite beautiful, patted the mattress.

"Come back to bed, Samantha."

I looked at the woman; her inviting lips upturned into a flirtatious smile. She patted the mattress again. Even through my groggy haze and pounding headache, I could see why she was so attractive - her smooth skin and shapely curves were undeniable. But I knew she couldn't stay; I had work in an hour and this wasn't a situation I wanted to waste any more time on.

Reluctantly, I tore my gaze away from the stranger and turned back to my clothes. "Sorry," I started, not knowing what else to say. "You, um, need to get going."

The woman didn't move.

I nervously glanced at the clock; I had to be at work in less than an hour. This woman was definitely not a part of my plan for today, and I wanted her out of my apartment as soon as possible.

"Um, sorry, I really must get ready for work," I said, trying my best to sound polite but firm. The stranger seemed unfazed by my rejection.

"Last night was amazing," she purred. "Can I come back soon?"

I inwardly groaned; this wasn't getting any easier. How

could I politely ask the stranger to leave without saying the wrong thing? Desperately, I racked my brain, but all I could come up with was an awkward silence that seemed to stretch on forever.

Finally, the woman sighed and grabbed her clothes from the floor. Her actions were still slow and seductive as she dressed herself before walking towards me with a victorious smirk.

"My name is Sarah, by the way," she said, then pecked me on the cheek. "I programmed my number into your phone. Call me if you want another unbelievable night."

After deleting Sarah's number, I quickly showered, changed, and slugged back aspirin and coffee.

"This has to stop," I groaned, forcing my feet into a pair of blue leather flats. There was no way I'd survive in heels today.

I looked at myself in the mirror, taking in the unflattering reflection. My usually neat and tidy hair was dishevelled, my eyes bloodshot from lack of sleep, and my clothes wrinkled from last night's escapade.

I hadn't sold a single property in months, and my boss Charlotte was getting twitchy about it. She knew we all had rough patches, but this was ridiculous. Before her girlfriend Julianna started at ICE, I'd been the number one realtor. Now I was dead last. It was time to put an end to my reckless nights out and focus on what mattered - selling properties and making money.

With a heavy sigh, I grabbed my Gucci laptop bag from its spot near the door and made my way out into the early morning sunlight. The fresh air felt good against my skin, but it did nothing to boost my spirits or quell the feeling of dread growing inside of me with every step forward. Nothing short of a miracle would save me now; there had to be something more than luck in store for me if I wanted to get back on top.

The morning rush hour traffic in Los Angeles was a nightmare, as usual. I felt my temper rising with every red light, every honk and every driver that cut me off.

I glanced at the clock on my dashboard and groaned. It was already past ten, more than an hour after my usual arrival time. Charlotte would be angry with me for sure, but there was nothing I could do besides drive faster and hope for the best.

My mind wandered back to last night's antics as I inched forward in the sea of cars. That woman Sarah was only one of many strangers I'd slept with in recent months - something completely out of character for me. I usually hated being touched by people I didn't know, so why did I suddenly crave it? Was it my fragile ego that drove me to these desperate, furtive encounters? Or some darker need to put my own problems aside and not have to think about myself?

No matter how hard I tried, it just didn't seem to help; I hadn't sold a single property in months. My career was going downhill fast and my boss, Charlotte, was getting more frustrated with me for not meeting her expectations. She'd warned us all- nobody's job was guaranteed, and we were expected to produce results or else face the consequences. It seemed like now might be the time when those consequences would come back to haunt me if my luck didn't change soon.

The thought made my stomach churn, and a wave of nausea swept over me as I finally pulled into the parking lot at

ICE Realty. Taking a deep breath, I grabbed my laptop bag from the passenger seat and stepped out of the car.

Today had to be different - it had to be better than all of yesterday's disasters and failures combined if there was any chance of saving my career.

I walked into the glass and steel offices of Iconic California Estates with my head held high, determined to make this day better than the last. My coworkers, Lucy and Kim, were already at their desks, scrolling through emails and typing away on their computers. They nodded in my direction as I passed them but said nothing; they were used to my late arrivals by now.

Just outside the entrance, the office manager, Gray, was seated at his desk. He looked up at me with a disapproving glare before speaking.

"You're really pushing things today, Samantha. I can't keep making excuses to Charlotte for you." His words made me cringe; he was right, of course - I couldn't be so unprofessional, especially when I hadn't sold a fucking house in months.

I took a deep breath and gave him a curt nod before heading towards the breakroom. A cup of steaming hot coffee might be enough to jolt me awake.

"Looks like somebody had a good time last night."

Damn it. I poured coffee into my mug and slowly turned around.

"Good morning, Julianna." I nodded in her direction and forced myself to stroll slowly out of the breakroom. I had nothing against her, but now that she and Charlotte were involved, I felt like I had someone else to hide from when I felt like hell.

When I got to my office, I put my bag down on the desk and flopped in my chair.

"Why does it feel like something bad is going to happen?" I muttered.

I opened my laptop with a sigh, already suspecting what I was going to find. Sure enough, the calendar notification was right there in front of me—my noon appointment to show the Rampling estate had been canceled.

"Fuck me."

It felt like a slap in the face; yet another sign that I was failing at this job. The idea that someone else at another firm had sold the estate before I even had a chance to show it angered me. It seemed no matter how hard I tried, I couldn't catch a break in the real estate business - and it was taking its toll.

My stomach churned as I remembered all the past few months' disasters and failures. It seemed like every day I was one step closer to being fired from this job, and now this?

I let out a frustrated groan and slammed the laptop shut. It wasn't too late though—maybe if I worked extra hard over the next few days, things would turn around for me and Charlotte wouldn't have any other choice than to keep me on board.

I had to try; it was my last hope—so with one final deep breath, I opened up my laptop again and got back to work.

"Knock knock."

I glanced up to see Gray in the doorway. He'd recently bleached his hair platinum, and I wasn't used to it yet.

"May I?" He gestured toward the leather wingback chair in front of my desk.

"Knock yourself out, Gray." I muttered, knowing he was going to read me the riot act.

"Samantha." He settled into the chair and looked me in the eye. "You've had a shitty few months, but I think I can help you get back on track." He smiled. "I've got a lead for you. A Broadway star just moved to town, and she's looking for a home."

"Broadway stars aren't movie-star rich," I mumbled. "But I guess I can't be choosy, huh?"

"Nope, you can't." Gray slid a folder across the desk. "But maybe this will help you get back into the groove again." He nodded at the folder. "Go on, open it."

I reluctantly opened the folder, expecting to see some unknown Broadway actor. But when I glanced inside, my heart stopped. There was the name of the only woman I'd ever loved.

My hands trembled as I flipped through the details in the folder, feeling anger and confusion welling up inside me. What was she doing here? And why was Gray so eager for me to work with her?

These questions raced through my head as I tried to keep my composure.

"Is something wrong, Samantha?"

I glanced up at Gray and forced a smiled. "No, but perhaps a different agent would work better with this particular client."

"You don't have any other clients right now, and the other agents are busy." Gray stood up and went to the door. "Samantha, do yourself a favor." He shook his head slowly back and forth, then sighed. "Dry out. And no, I don't think you're an alcoholic or anything like that. But something's been off with you lately, and Charlotte's beginning to be concerned. I'm setting up a meeting with this client for next Monday. That gives you an entire weekend to sober up and get rested. I virtually guarantee you'll be able to sell this woman the house of her dreams if you do as I tell you."

"You're not my boss," I snapped.

"No, but I am your friend." Gray glanced at his watch. "Charlotte and Julianna are leaving in an hour for the airport, and they'll be gone the rest of the day. Once they're gone, why don't you leave early?" He shrugged. "Get some rest, and when you meet with the client Monday morning, you'll be ready to hit a home run, okay?"

"Fine."

As soon as Gray left, I was filled with dread. "Why you?" I stared at the paperwork in front of me. "Do you know that it's me you're going to be working with, Morgan?"

Chapter Three
Morgan

I stepped into the rehearsal room, and my heart skipped a beat. It was finally happening, my big Hollywood break. I felt a nervous excitement bubbling inside me as I looked around the room.

My gaze lingered on the group of people gathered around the long table at the center of the room. These were my co-stars for the upcoming movie, *Echoes of Elysium*. Some of them I recognized from New York, others I had only seen in magazines.

"Morgan?"

I swiveled my head around, trying to find the woman who'd spoken to me. Across the room, I saw the director, Eva Thorne.

"Welcome to bedlam!" She crossed the room and air kissed both of my cheeks. "Take a seat wherever you like. Oh, have you eaten yet? We have a small buffet in the corner." She pointed at a table laden with food and drinks, then jogged off.

I found an empty chair and sat down, feeling my palms

grow sweaty. I glanced up and caught a few of my co-stars looking at me, and quickly averted my gaze. It always took me a few days before I felt comfortable around new people.

"Hey, love."

I glanced up and saw my Broadway co-star, Billy Grant.

"Is this seat taken?" He pointed to the chair next to mine.

"No, it's not. Hey, would you mind grabbing me a bottle of seltzer before you sit down? I forgot, and..."

"Anything for you, sweety." Billy strolled over to the buffet and grabbed two bottles. He was the easiest actor I'd ever worked with. None of that method acting bullshit. He always knew his lines and had already been nominated for three Tony awards. Like me, this was his first major Hollywood film role.

"Are you nervous?" Billy whispered as he sat next to me.

Before I could answer, Eva Thorne cleared her throat and sat across from us.

"Alright, let's get started," she said firmly. "I first want to thank Morgan Sterling and Billy Grant for recreating their Broadway roles for the screen. Without their talents, this project would never have gotten off the ground."

Our co-stars politely applauded, and I felt my face flush.

"Morgan, Billy, you're probably wondering why you need to be at a read through of the screenplay since you've played these characters so many times." Eva took off her black-framed glasses and eyed us. "It's because we had to rewrite a few of the scenes to make it work better for film. Plus, this is an excellent chance for you two to get to know your new co-stars better." Eva smiled, then snapped her fingers. An assistant passed out the scripts, and once everyone had a copy, Eva opened hers.

"Let's start at the beginning." The sound of pages turning filled the room. "The story follows Elizabeth and William as they throw caution to the wind and take a chance on lasting love," Eva explained. "It's an epic romance set against the backdrop of a quaint coastal town and its surrounding beauty."

She paused briefly to take a sip from her water bottle before continuing. "There are moments of raw emotion, love scenes, and even some heartbreaking drama," she said as her gaze traveled around the room. "But most importantly, there's hope that true love can conquer all."

I felt tears prick my eyes, imagining how this story would look on film. Eva had perfectly captured the emotion of a summer romance, and I couldn't wait to bring it to life.

"Let's begin the read through." Eva pointed at me. "Morgan has the first line."

I glanced around the room, then took a deep breath before reading it aloud.

"We've only just met," I said, my voice shaking slightly. "Why do I feel like we've known each other for far longer?"

"Excuse me?" Billy winked at me. "I just want to know who the artist is?"

"Oh, that's me." I noticed Eva had shortened the line from the original play. "I'm Elizabeth Pryor."

"You're very talented, but I don't know much about art." Billy read the line perfectly. "My name is William, and I'm staying at the Oyster Bay Bed And Breakfast. May I buy you a drink sometime?"

* * *

After the reading was finished, I felt relieved. Yes, the screenplay departed from the original script, but they'd done an excellent job of it.

I glanced over at Billy, who flashed me a smile before gathering his things to leave.

Eva clapped her hands together and thanked us all for coming. "We're going to make an amazing movie," she declared as we filed out of the room.

As soon as I stepped outside, I felt like I could finally breathe again. Everything had gone well, and hopefully the film shoot would be just as smooth.

"Did you get a rental yet?" Billy called out from across the parking lot. Did he mean an apartment, or a car? I must have looked confused, because he laughed. "The better question is, do you need a ride?"

"Oh." I shielded my eyes from the bright afternoon sun. "I'm a city girl, and don't have a license. Hey, do you want to grab a drink with me? I don't know why, but the reading kind of stressed me out."

"I can't." Billy pressed a button on his key fob, and I heard a car's doors unlock. "Patty is at the apartment with the kids, and I'm sure she needs a break. But I'll drop you off at my favorite bar. It's only a few blocks from here."

Did I really want my co-star to think I drank alone?

"What the hell." I grinned. "Thanks for the lift, but I expect you and your charming wife to go out drinking with me soon."

I stepped inside The Rainbow Bar & Grill, my stomach turning in anticipation. I hadn't been to a bar alone since I was in college, and it felt weird and exciting all at once. Taking a deep breath, I scanned the room, looking for an empty booth.

My gaze landed on one tucked away in the corner near the window, and I quickly made my way over there. Sliding into the seat, I ordered a whiskey sour before taking out my phone to check for messages.

There were three messages from Rob, but I didn't feel like talking to my agent just yet. I'm sure he just wanted to know how the read through went, but I was in the mood to reflect on it alone.

The whiskey sour went down smoothly, and I felt my anxiety from earlier fade away. The read-through had gone surprisingly well, considering the fact that we were working with a new script. Everyone was in sync and had brought their A-Game.

The bar was dark inside, but there were plenty of people chatting animatedly at tables throughout the room. I felt completely at ease, and it allowed me to reflect on the reading earlier without any distractions.

Of course, Billy and I knew our parts. For eight performances a week for close to a year, we'd portrayed Elizabeth and William at the Shubert Theatre in New York. The other actors were all new to the story, but I assumed they all wanted the movie to succeed as much as we did. My only complaint was how they'd shortened our lines. Lengthy dialogs were replaced by smoldering stares at a camera.

I'd done a lot of work in European cinema, thanks to my extended family in Romania. Because of that, I knew how to adjust my acting techniques for the camera. Poor Billy was in for a rude awakening. This was his first movie, and the way a story is told on film differs vastly from on stage.

"He's a pro," I muttered to myself, then waved at a passing waitress. "Another whiskey sour, please."

A sudden commotion near the door had me turning to see what was going on. A tall figure dressed in a sharp suit and black coat strode in with an entourage of paparazzi following close behind. The manager quickly shooed them away, but not before one managed to snap a few photos.

The man stopped at the bar, and I noticed how handsome he was as he ordered a drink. His face was familiar, though I wasn't sure where I'd seen him before. Then it hit me: Jude Evans. He was one of the hottest actors in Hollywood right now.

My heart skipped a beat as he turned to look around the room, his gaze eventually coming to rest on me. We locked eyes for what felt like an eternity until one of his handlers cleared his throat and gestured towards a private room off to the side. Jude nodded and made his way over there with an air of confidence that made it seem like he owned the place.

Jude walked past me, then stopped in his tracks. He slowly spun around, then a smile spread across his cheeks. A moment later, he was standing next to my table.

"Aren't you Morgan Popescu?"

My eyes slid from the side of his face to the curve of his lips and along his chiseled jaw. I wasn't into guys at all, but for Jude, I'd make an exception.

"Yes, though now I'm known as Morgan Sterling." I smiled.

"I was in Rome shooting a movie and I watched a series you were in." He tapped his chin a few times. "I think it was called, *Procesele lui Mary*."

He'd butchered the pronunciation, but why mention it?

"You were amazing in it. Every night after shooting, I'd

watch a few episodes." Jude gestured toward the other side of the booth. "May I join you for a drink?"

"It would be a pleasure."

Jude took off his jacket and handed it to a young man in his twenties, probably his personal assistant.

The waitress rushed over and stammered, "Mr. Evans, we have a private room available so you can..."

"I'm going to have a drink with this lovely lady first, then I'll join the rest of my team in the private room you've so thoughtfully provided us." There was a subtle sarcastic sound to his voice. "I'll have a vodka on the rocks, top shelf. Carter," Jude nodded at his assistant. "Please join the rest of the team, and I'll be with you all in a few minutes."

The assistant scampered off, and Jude's self-assurance mesmerized me. Was this what it was like to be such an enormous star? To snap your fingers and everyone runs to do your bidding? If that was the case, sign me up.

The waitress dropped off Jude's drink. Then he flashed his famous blue eyes at me. "What brings you to Hollywood?"

"They're making the film version of a play I starred in on Broadway." I sipped my drink, wondering if this movie star was about to hit on me. According to the gossip sites, he was involved with another A-lister, Lorna Baker. "It's called Echoes of Elysium."

"Oh, I saw the touring show here at the Pantages Theatre. But I don't recall seeing you in it. Trust me, I wouldn't have forgotten that." Jude winked, and I bit my lip to keep from laughing. For the first time in my life, a major movie star was hitting on me, and of course, he was a man.

"Who's your lady friend, Jude?"

"Fuck." Jude muttered. The dreaded paparazzi began snapping shots of Jude and me.

The restaurant staff saw what was happening and sprung into action. "Get out!" One of the servers screamed. The scummy asshole ran out of the restaurant, leaving us alone once again.

Jude turned to me with a sheepish grin on his face. "I'm so sorry about that," he said apologetically. "This is why I try to avoid public places." He sighed heavily, then stood up from the booth. "I should probably go meet my team now."

"Nice to meet you, Jude," I purred.

Was this really my life now? Did I just have a drink with one of Hollywood's biggest stars?

"Miss, we're so sorry about that." The waitress came back to my table and placed a fresh drink in front of me. "We're taking care of your bill."

I picked up the drink and realized I was already buzzed. But I couldn't tell if it was from the booze or from the attention Jude paid me. One thing was for sure. I wanted what he had. The fame and money was what I'd always craved. But I didn't want the rest of the bullshit. For Christ's sake, the man couldn't even go out for a fucking drink without being hounded by the press.

My phone buzzed, and I saw my agent's name flash across the screen.

"Hi Ron," I felt my lips twisting in amusement. "I just had a cocktail with Jude Evans."

"What?" Ron gasped, and I giggled. "Please tell me there were cameras around."

"Oh yes, the paps follow the poor man everywhere he goes. Hopefully, you'll see pictures of us online within a few hours. Gotta love free publicity." I glanced up at the entrance, and through the window I saw at least a dozen people milling about with cameras. Was I prepared for real stardom? Because the thought of being chased day in and day out by those horrible people made my skin crawl.

"You're making my job easy, Morgan." Rob laughed. "The reason I'm calling is to let you know I set up an appointment with a realtor on Monday morning. Oh, and I just thought of something. Do you want to learn how to drive?"

I pondered the question. I had no particular desire to learn, having grown accustomed to being chauffeured. "Not particularly," I responded. "What time is the appointment, and with whom?"

"Ten, and hold on a second," Rob said, and I heard him shuffling papers. "The firm is Iconic California Estates. I'll message you the details."

After I hung up, I watched the commotion outside the bar and considered the whirlwind of events that had just unfolded.

Would my newfound fame and success come at a cost I wasn't prepared to pay?

Chapter Four
Samantha

"Good morning, Samantha." Gray smiled as I strolled into the office. "How was your weekend? Did you rest up for your big appointment this morning?" His smile stretched from ear to ear, and I wondered if he'd found a new boyfriend. He always acted eager to please when he was getting laid regularly.

I stood in front of his desk, crossed my arms over my chest, and forced a grin onto my face. "It was peachy."

"Aw, c'mon Samantha. You had almost three full days to rest up. Did you take my advice and lay off the sauce?" He took off his tortoiseshell glasses and eyed me. "I'm just trying to..."

"Yes, Gray." I looked up at the ceiling. "I haven't touched a drop since last Thursday night. On Saturday, I went to the spa and had a massage and a pedicure. Sunday, I jogged on the beach by the Santa Monica pier. I feel so wholesome it makes want to puke." I added the last part so I wouldn't sound like a wuss. "Let me get some coffee, then

I'll prepare for the client." I turned to go to the break room, then called out over my shoulder. "Thanks for being my friend, Gray."

After grabbing a cup of coffee, I hurried to my office and shut the door.

"Swear to God, if this is really Morgan, my Morgan, I'm going to lose it." I sat behind my desk and steepled my fingers under my chin. What I'd told Gray was true. I'd gone to the spa, went jogging on the beach, and didn't touch a drop of booze. But I'd also obsessed over Morgan.

"Hell, she probably doesn't remember me," I sighed.

I couldn't help but feel a twinge of excitement as I thought about seeing her again. I hadn't seen or spoken to her since I left Teeterville after our junior year of high school. She didn't know that I'd become a successful realtor working with celebrities and the elite of Hollywood. What would she think when she saw how far I'd come?

A part of me was anxious to find out what emotions Morgan still harbored toward me. Did she still think of me in the same way? Did she ever forgive me for ghosting her without any explanation or closure? It was a terrifying thought and one that kept me up most of the weekend.

But there was nothing to do now except prepare for our meeting and try not to make a fool out of myself in front of Morgan. I needed to stay focused and make sure this meeting went well, no matter what happened between us personally.

"I need the money too much to fuck this up."

My heart raced as I switched on my desktop computer and searched for the file with potential homes to show Morgan.

I'd been mentally preparing for this meeting all weekend. But nothing could have prepped me for the wave of emotions that overcame me when I thought about seeing her again after all these years.

After finding the file, I pulled out the brochures and other paperwork and almost laughed out loud when I realized my hands were shaking. "No more coffee for me," I muttered under my breath as I set everything up neatly on my desk.

I knew it was crucial that I keep this meeting professional no matter what happened between us personally. If Morgan made a decision based purely on business, then maybe we could both come out of this ahead.

But as much as I told myself that, in the back of my mind, there was still the question gnawing away at me: what did Morgan really think of me? Did she even remember our past? Would she forgive me for leaving without explanation?

"Only time will tell," I muttered. "Hell, it might not be her. It could be someone else entirely."

But I knew in my gut it was my Morgan. Would she ever forgive me?

The intercom buzzed, and I nearly jumped out of my skin.

"Ms. Sterling is here." Gray announced.

I'd swear there was a shark living in my gut, and it just took a bite out of my newly sober liver.

Pushing the button on the intercom, I replied, "Be there shortly, Gray."

I looked at my reflection in the full-length mirror hanging on the back of the closet door and sighed. My makeup was perfect, as always, but I could see the strain in my eyes from lack of sleep.

I shook my head to clear it before applying a final layer of lipstick and giving my hair one last brush. I took a deep breath and slowly exhaled.

It was time to face my past.

My heart pounded in my chest as I strolled down the corridor to meet Morgan. Every step felt like it took an eternity, and I could feel tension in the air.

As I rounded the corner, I saw her standing in front of Gray's desk. They were making small talk, which gave me a few seconds to observe her. She'd changed so much since I'd last seen her, but there was still something familiar about her that tugged at my heartstrings. Obviously, she was much more sophisticated now. Her emerald green eyes were still captivating, and her presence filled the room with energy. Oh yes, she's a Broadway actress now, and you could literally feel her star power.

"Ms. Sterling," I murmured, and held out my hand.

Morgan's mouth dropped open.

Shit. She recognizes me. I don't know whether to hug her or run screaming from the office.

"Do you two know each other?" Gray asked.

Morgan's lips twisted, then she slowly reached out and took my hand. "Samantha Bishop. What a surprise."

Gray cleared his throat. "Samantha, would you like me to bring some coffee and pastries to your office?"

I opened my mouth, but nothing came out. Finally, Morgan turned to Gray and replied for me.

"That would be lovely." Morgan smiled, and an image of her laughing as we cut class back in high school filled my head. "I forgot to eat breakfast. I'm so anxious to find my new home."

"I'll bring it right away," Gray said, then he stood up and left.

We stared into each other's eyes for what seemed like forever. Finally, I was able to speak.

"Morgan, please, come with me to my office."

I walked away from Gray's desk and headed towards my office, Morgan following closely behind. As we rounded the corner, I could feel her eyes taking in every detail of our surroundings. Though it was clear she'd changed since high school, the curiosity in those bright green eyes hadn't changed one bit.

We arrived at my office, and I motioned for her to take a seat on the couch. The atmosphere was thick with tension as we both struggled to find something to say. Finally, I mustered up the courage to speak.

"What kind of home are you looking for?" I sat on the couch next to her, though I left plenty of space between us. "There are some excellent homes in the valley, or perhaps you'd be interested in a penthouse overlooking the ocean?"

Morgan licked her red lips.

"Here you are ladies," Gray sauntered in and placed a silver tray on the coffee table in front of us. "Will there be anything else, Samantha?"

"No, thanks," I mumbled. Gray left, shutting the door behind him. I poured a cup of coffee for myself, then remembered my hands shaking earlier. "Here, Morgan."

She took the cup and sipped it. "Thanks."

God, this was so awkward. "Please, have a pastry."

Morgan lifted a brow, and I realized my southern accent, which I'd spent years getting rid of, had come back full force. But I couldn't help it. Something about this woman made me forget who and what I'd become. All I could do was stare at her, because Father Time apparently loved this woman. She was even more stunning than I remembered. Morgan cleared her throat, pulling me out of my trance-like state.

"So what brings you to Los Angeles?"

Morgan placed her coffee cup on the table and smiled. "I'm making my first Hollywood feature film. It's based on a play I performed on Broadway."

"Oh, isn't that delightful?" I forced a smile to my face, but inwardly cringed. Jesus, I sounded like my grandmother. "I wish you all the success in the world."

Tension filled the air between us. Damn it, just keep things professional, and everything will be okay. Hell, maybe I should deliberately fuck this up so she'll go to another realtor.

"Samantha Bishop." Morgan slowly stated my name, then shocked me by reaching over the cushion in between us and taking my hand.

"What the hell happened to you after junior year? It's like you vanished from the face of the earth."

Chapter Five
Samantha

"I, um..."

"You can trust me, Samantha." Morgan tightened her grip on my hand. "Remember when we promised we'd be friends forever? Well, I meant it. It appears to me that something bad happened, otherwise you'd have told me by now."

How could I tell Morgan? This is the first time in twenty years we've seen each other. Why would I share such a painful part of my past with someone who was now almost a stranger?

"Honestly, Morgan, it's not a big deal." I forced myself to smile. "My parents sent me to live with some relatives in Mississippi for my senior year. And after I graduated, I moved to California." What I didn't mention was that I'd never spoken to my family again. Oh, and I didn't have relatives in Mississippi either. It was a girls' home, or rather, a naughty girls' home, if you believed the crazy bible thumpers who owned it.

Morgan's brow furrowed. She opened her mouth, then shut it again.

"Let's narrow down the type of home you're interested in. Maybe after I show you a few properties, we can go out for a drink and catch up." My cheek muscles were beginning to hurt from this never ending fake smile. Oh, and I'd promised myself to lay off the booze for a while. Well, a drink didn't have to involve alcohol. Aren't there a few sober bars around town?

"Samantha, it's been years since we last saw each other." Morgan let go of my hand. "I'm going to be in Los Angeles for the foreseeable future, and I need a friend. You, my agent, and a couple of actors are the only people I know. It would be wonderful to hang out with someone not in the entertainment industry."

I bit my lower lip and felt a flush racing up my neck. This woman was more stunning than the girl I left behind in Georgia. Would she want something more than friendship?

"I have a list of properties to show you, Morgan. Let's take care of that first, then I'll take you out for a drink."

"I'm glad we reconnected, Samantha," Morgan purred, her voice dropping an octave. Her fingers traced the back of my hand, sending shivers up my arm. "Remember when we were young and reckless? Innocent promises whispered under the glow of summer stars?" The memory of us tangled in white cotton sheets flickered in my mind's eye. Morgan was the first woman I'd ever been with, and images of those few nights we'd been together raced through my mind.

"I remember," I choked out, my throat feeling impossibly tight. Did she know my heart was pounding a fierce tattoo against my breastbone? Could she hear it over the thrumming silence that enveloped us? Oh God, I couldn't handle this right now. I must steer the conversation back to business. I stood up and did my best imitation of being a competent realtor.

"Come. Let's go look at some houses."

* * *

Morgan and I stood in the foyer of a stunning Beverly Hills mansion two blocks from Rodeo Drive. The previous owner had spared no expense in decorating it. Marble flooring, crystal chandeliers, and art from around the world adorned the walls. The view of the city could be seen through the immense windows that lined one wall of the living room.

It was clear Morgan was impressed with what she saw. She strolled from room to room, pausing to admire each piece of artwork or piece of furniture along the way.

"This is amazing," she said as we made our way back to the living room. "I've never seen such luxury before."

"It's beautiful," I agreed, trying not to show my surprise at her enthusiasm. "Do you think you'd like to make this your new home?"

Morgan laughed. "I'm sorry to waste your time, but I'm sure this place is out of my price range. Most of my career has been in Europe and on Broadway. Neither pays as well as starring in a Marvel movie."

Her green eyes caught mine, and for a moment, I regretted not flirting with her in my office. If I wasn't mistaken, she found me as attractive as I did her.

"I have a lovely penthouse to show you in West Hollywood." I walked to the front door and opened it. "Three bedrooms, a study, and a stunning view of the city. I think it'll fit your budget."

Morgan sauntered up to me, then took my hand. "I'm sorry if I was too forward in your office. Normally I don't behave that way, but seeing you again has brought back so many memories."

"Good ones, I hope." Jesus, I sounded like an idiot.

"Yes, all of my memories of you are wonderful. Except for one." Morgan let go of my hand. "The day I went to your house, and your parents said you were gone. Can you believe they slammed the door in my face?"

"Unfortunately, yes." I stepped outside and Morgan followed behind me. I locked the door, then walked toward my car. "I haven't spoken to them since then. They've never reached out to me, and I've never wanted them to."

We got in my car, and I started the engine.

"You're a survivor, Samantha." Morgan sighed. "Strong and resilient. Now, show me this magnificent penthouse and maybe afterward we can make up for lost time."

The drive to the penthouse was silent, but the tension between us seemed to increase with each passing mile. I could feel Morgan's gaze on me as I navigated the streets, but I was too nervous to meet her eyes. I remembered what it was like when we were together, and the thought of revisiting that part of my life filled me with a mixture of excitement and dread. I wasn't the same girl anymore, and she'd changed too.

When we arrived at the building, I took a deep breath before hopping out of the car. Morgan followed close behind me as we ascended the stairs to the front door.

"Hi Samantha." A man stepping out of the elevator

greeted me as we stepped inside. The door shut, and Morgan winked at me.

"You're popular. Who's that guy?"

"I sold him a condo on the third floor." I pressed the button for the penthouse. "His name slips my mind."

The elevator began its ascent, and a few moments later it stopped. I pulled out my key, then stuck it into the lock under the button for the penthouse. "As you can see, it's very secure. You'd be the only person with a key to the top floor."

"Ooh, fancy." Morgan purred. Then the elevator doors opened, and we stepped into the apartment.

The living room was spacious and bright, with floor-to-ceiling windows that overlooked the Hollywood Hills in stunning detail. The furniture was modern yet inviting, and the artwork gave it a sophisticated yet homey feel. We continued through every room, admiring all of its features along the way.

"This is perfect," Morgan said as she stopped in front of the window in the primary bedroom. "I can imagine waking up here every morning."

"The view is truly magnificent, isn't it?" I said, standing next to Morgan, who was still peering out the window.

"Indeed, just like you," she replied with a coy smile.

Her compliment caught me off guard, as did her hand that found its way to mine. Her fingers entwined gently around mine, her grip soft but firm.

Morgan turned to face me, and her green eyes sparkled with a heat that made my heart pound in my chest. Without saying a word, she leaned in closer, eliminated the distance between us. The scent of her perfume - sweet and spicy - filled my senses. My breath hitched when her lips met mine in a slow kiss. It wasn't rushed or frantic; instead, it was slow and determined, each moment loaded with meaning.

We broke apart slowly, gasping for air. Morgan's gaze locked onto mine again, blazing with desire. "Would you like to continue this in a more private setting?"

Chapter Six
Morgan

"Morgan, you're a very attractive woman. And if my lips are to be believed, an even better kisser than I remembered." Samantha stepped back and took a deep breath. "But I'm kind of going through some stuff right now. If you're still interested in getting a drink, I'm game."

My cheeks burned. "I don't know what came over me. When I saw you again, it all came rushing back. The memories of me and you, and well, it's overwhelming." I slowly turned around and walked to the elevator door. It was rare for me to come on to anyone, and even though she'd rebuffed my advances, I suspected she was just as attracted to me as I was to her. Perhaps Samantha really was going through something, something deep.

"Are you coming?" I called over my shoulder, then heard the sound of Samantha's heels crossing the parquet floor. "I'm thirsty, and a cocktail would really hit the spot."

"That would be lovely." Samantha murmured, and the elevator doors slid open. "After you."

The elevator car descended, and the tension between us was palpable. Samantha stood a few feet away from me, her eyes fixed on the floor of the car as we made our way down to the lobby. I couldn't help but steal glances at her as she stood there, her face illuminated by the faint overhead light.

Time seemed to slow as my heart raced faster with each passing second. I wanted so badly to reach out and touch her, to feel that same electric spark I'd felt when I'd kissed her upstairs. But I knew better than to push things too far.

Finally, after what seemed like an eternity, we stepped out into the lobby.

"So, where are we going now?" I asked, and I noticed for the first time the slight bluish tint under Samantha's eyes. Lack of sleep?

"I know the perfect spot. It's called the Velvet Vixen, and since it's early, we shouldn't have any problems talking about old times."

The Velvet Vixen had a welcoming feel about it. The walls were painted black, and the furniture was upholstered in deep, luxurious red velvet. I could see pairs of women gathered around tables, talking and laughing.

"My first Hollywood lesbian bar." I smiled at Samantha, who led me to a booth in the corner. I slid into one side while she took the opposite side. We were both quiet for a moment, then Samantha spoke up.

"Tell me everything. It must be an exciting life, acting in

your first feature film." She flipped her blonde hair over her shoulder, and I noticed her gaze wouldn't meet mine.

"It's been..."

"Welcome to the Velvet Vixen." A short waitress with a black crew cut interrupted us. "Howdy Samantha. What can I get you two to drink?"

"I'll have a glass of merlot." I leaned back in the booth and nodded toward Samantha.

"A Mango Tango would really hit the spot, Tracy." Samantha apparently knew the server. "Oh, and hold the rum. I'm in the mood for a virgin."

The server tilted her head and eyed Samantha for a moment. "You want a virgin Mango Tango?"

I watched as blood raced up Samantha's neck.

"Yes, Tracy. It's Monday afternoon, and my liver needs a long rest." Samantha turned back to me and grinned. "I've been going through a slump at work, and figured now was as good a time as any to get healthy. I'm going to a yoga class tomorrow evening, and I'm getting a facial on Wednesday."

The server laughed, then raced to the next table.

"Do you know her?" I pointed at the server. She was very hot, if you were into skater chicks.

"We had a brief fling a few weeks ago." Samantha frowned. "Actually, I've had a lot of little flings lately. I'm attempting a reset. No more booze, and no more meaningless, um, encounters." Samantha's brow furrowed. "Shit, I'm sorry. We're just getting to know each other again, and I'm probably sharing too much."

"Hey, it's okay." I reached across the table and patted her hand. "And your slump at work is over. I want that penthouse, so start the paperwork. Living in hotels gets really old after a while. For the first time in years, I'm in a place where I can establish some roots." I was curious about what else was going on with Samantha.

"So tell me what's been going on," I said tentatively. "Is it really just work?"

I was curious. She'd stopped drinking and whoring around, which was definitely a good thing, but it seemed like there was more she wasn't telling me. It made me feel a little uneasy—I knew how hard it can be to navigate loneliness. It was like being lost at sea, without a compass or a map.

She sighed heavily and looked down at her hands. "It's more than that," she breathed. She looked up at me with an expression of fear and resignation in her eyes. "I'm trying to get over something from my past."

"Here's your merlot, and a virgin Mango Tango for Samantha." The server placed our drinks down and scampered off. Samantha placed her face in her hands for a moment, then looked up at the ceiling.

"No matter how much I try to move on, it's like my heart won't let go of the pain," she continued, her voice breaking slightly as emotion overcame her. "Sometimes I feel like nothing will ever make me happy again."

A tear slid down her cheek, and she quickly wiped it away with the back of her hand. Instinctively, I reached up to brush away the evidence of sorrow before anyone else noticed, but then pulled my hand back. Samantha took a sip of her drink. "This is much better without the rum. And I'm sorry for dumping this on you, because..."

"Stop it." I picked up my glass and swirled the wine around. "I wouldn't be here if I didn't want to be. After all, it's not every day I'm reunited with the first girl I cared for. So tell me, what really happened? Why did you disappear?"

Samantha's voice was barely a whisper as she spoke. "Billy Turner happened."

The words hung in the air, heavy with emotion and pain. I could see the tears welling up in her eyes, but she refused to let them fall. I felt my heart break for her, for all the pain she'd been through, and I wanted to tell her that everything was going to be ok—even though I knew it wouldn't be.

"Wasn't he your boyfriend?" I asked, and a bolt of jealousy shot through me. We'd kept our relationship secret from everyone in Teeterville. Whenever Samantha and that stupid jock went out on a date, I'd suffer in silence.

"Don't you remember?" Samantha's voice trembled. "I dated him to keep my parents off my back about you. My folks thought you were this exotic European flower hellbent on corrupting me. Billy's family was a big deal in that shithole of a town. As long as I was dating him, they thought everything was peachy."

"I hated him." The words flew out of my mouth before I could stop them. "Sorry, but..."

"Not as much as I do." Samantha grimaced.

I stood up and sat next to her. "He...?" I whispered, unable to bring myself to say it out loud.

Samantha nodded sadly. "He raped me in the back of his pickup truck. He justified it by saying we'd be married soon, so we might as well fuck." Tears streamed down her face as she spoke, and she quickly wiped them away with the back of her hand. "When it was over, he just drove away, leaving me next to Lake Lewis."

She shuddered and looked up at me with eyes full of pain

and sorrow. Without thinking, I reached out to put an arm around her shoulders in comfort. She leaned into me and sobbed silently for a few moments before pulling away.

"After that," she said softly, "I knew I had to get out of Teeterville if I ever wanted to move on with my life. My folks blamed me for the rape when I told them. Then they sent me to this group home in Mississippi, and when I turned eighteen, I caught a bus for LA and never looked back."

"Oh baby, I'm so, so, sorry."

As I watched Samantha cry, I was filled with remorse. I should have been there for her. She must have felt so alone and scared after that terrible experience. But instead of being by her side through it all, I'd judged her harshly, convinced that she left me because she didn't care about me.

I had no idea what she must have gone through—the fear, the shame, the pain of betrayal. I wanted to reach out and hold her close, to tell her it was going to be alright, but the words stuck in my throat like a lump of lead.

If only I had known about the rape sooner. If only I hadn't reacted so angrily when she left Teeterville without saying goodbye. But all those ifs didn't matter now—all that mattered was that this beautiful woman needed my comfort and reassurance more than ever before.

"What about you, Morgan?" Samantha straightened her shoulders and looked at me. "What happened to you after I left?"

Chapter Seven
Morgan

"Well, senior year was miserable." I began. "And I'm ashamed to say that I blamed you for it. You were gone, and your parents lied to my face about it."

"What did they say?" Samantha murmured, then she took my hand and squeezed it. "Actually, maybe I don't want to know. I haven't heard from them once, and despite the passage of time, it still hurts."

"What they said and did will only make your decision never to speak to them seem more valid." I took a long sip of wine. "I couldn't wait to see you after spending the summer at my grandmother's house. All day long I expected you to walk into class, sit next to me, and we'd whisper about our boring summer breaks."

"Mine was anything but boring," Samantha dryly remarked.

"After school, I debated whether I should go check on you. I mean, your parents didn't like me, I could tell. But I was feeling anxious, so I forced myself to go to your house. I knocked on their door and when they opened it, they looked me up and down with disdain. Your mother then spoke in a cold voice and said, 'What are you doing here?'

"What was she wearing?" Samantha asked, and for a moment, I was confused. "Please, it's important."

I shut my eyes for a moment, picturing the scene in my head. "If I recall correctly, I remember thinking your mom was dressed kind of weird. She piled her hair on her head, like a bouffant. And even though it was stifling outside, she had on a thick brown blouse buttoned all the way up to her neck, and long sleeves. Her skirt was the same muddy shade of brown, and it scraped the floor. The only pretty thing she wore was a gold cross hanging from her neck."

"My Uncle Vandy passed away in June, and he'd been a strict Pentecostal." Samantha swiped a tear away. "My parents left the Methodist church we'd always gone to, and they started going to his church. I think it was called the Graceful Flames Assembly. Anyhow, they dragged me along with them. They threw out all of my regular clothes and forced me to wear the same kind of outfit Mom wore. They'd always been strict, but as soon as they became Pentecostal, life became a living hell. Oh, and even though you were off at your grandmother's house in Europe, they forbade me from being friends with you. They said you were too worldly, or some other crap."

"They called you a whore," I whispered. My voice cracked as I spoke, and my throat ached. It was so much harder to say this than it had been to listen to her parents. Their words still rang in my ears, but they were muted now by the anger and hurt that seethed within me. "To my face, they called their own daughter a whore. To everyone's face, really. Then they said you wanted nothing to do with me. That you'd gone on some sort of Christian mission to make peace with God, and that they would pray for me."

"Then they slammed the door in your face, right?"

"After they told me that your faith and commitment to the church was much stronger than any friendship we ever had." I sighed. "Did they know about us?"

Samantha steepled her fingers under her chin. "No, and yes. Mom and Dad knew there was something deeper than friendship, but it never occurred to them that we were, you know, a couple." A little chuckle escaped her. "Honestly, I'm not sure they knew what an actual lesbian was. Or if they did, I didn't fit the stereotype of a butch woman looking to convert unsuspecting Christian girls. Plus, they thought I was a trollop, seducing Billy Turner so I could... never mind."

"What?"

"Nothing. It's all in the past now." Samantha drained the rest of her drink, and I wondered if she wished it had booze in it. "But the past keeps coming back to bite me in the ass."

Shit. "You don't mean me, do you?"

"No, sweet Jesus, no." Samantha shrugged, then placed a lock of blonde hair behind her ear. "I need to go to the bathroom. Would you mind letting me up?"

I stood, then sat on the other side of the booth while Samantha strolled away. She was hiding something; I was sure of it. But what right did I have to make her talk? It felt like I'd been punched in the gut and all the air had been knocked out of me. I'd always known that Samantha's parents were strict, but hearing her talk about it made me realize just how much they'd hurt her.

My mind strayed to the past, and I found myself thinking

about our relationship. She was my first love, but we'd never had the time or the emotional clarity to deal with it. Neither of us knew what we were doing back then, and we'd never done more than kiss and fondle each other. But this was something I wanted to explore further, because even after all these years, I was very attracted to her. But it felt wrong, like a betrayal of Samantha's hurt feelings.

Just then, she returned from the bathroom and sank down into the seat across from me. We simply looked at each other for a few moments before Samantha finally broke the silence.

"I'm shocked that I shared all that with you," she waved at the server, who came running over. "You're the first person I've ever spoken to about my past."

"Hey Samantha, you want something stronger this time? You look like you need it." Tracy smiled. Samantha had to be a good fifteen years older than the waitress, but she was such a knockout, it didn't matter. If I'd been the waitress, I couldn't have said no to a night or two in Samantha's bed.

"Nah, just give me another virgin Mango Tango." Samantha smiled at her.

"I'll take another merlot, please."

The server took off, and we stared at each other in silence for a long moment.

"So, are you in recovery now?" I asked, and Samantha giggled.

"No. But lately I've been partying too hard, and it's effecting my, well, everything." She shook her head back and forth a couple of times, then smiled. "Enough about me. What happened to you after high school?"

"After you left, I didn't want to stay in that hellhole. I knew I wanted to be an actress, so I filled out applications to

acting schools all over the country. Julliard showed some interest, and after I sent them an audition tape, they gave me a full
scholarship." I shut my eyes for a moment, remembering the
excitement of moving to New York. "But I only stayed for one
year. During a break, I'd gone back to Bucharest, and I audi-
tioned for a television series called Secretul Tinereții. That
means The Secret of Youth in English. When I got the part, I
decided to stay, and spent the next three years there. When the
show was cancelled, I kept auditioning for roles, and I ended
up being modestly successful."

"You're about to be in a feature film. That's wildly
successful in my book." Samantha winked, and my stomach
flipped. Jesus, I wish she was flirting with me.

"That was a long time coming." I leaned back and smiled.
"I'm 39 years old, and I'm finally cracking open Hollywood."

"And you're going to rule this town, I promise," Samantha
said, then the server dropped off our drinks and left. "Though
I'm not in the entertainment industry, I've met plenty of actors
through my job. Most of them burn bright for a few years, then
they go buy a ranch in Montana and disappear. What I
noticed is the vast majority of them get only one big break,
then they pick the wrong roles, or lose interest. Career actors
like yourself, the ones who've been working their entire lives in
the industry, are the ones who survive and thrive. So have
there been any long-term relationships?"

I blinked. That came out of left field.

"One." I sipped my merlot. "Her name was Juliette, and
we lived together for two years while I worked in Paris. At the
time, I struggled to find work, mostly because my French
sucked. But I was in love with her and determined to make our
relationship work. So I modeled, walking the runways of

Balenciaga, Dior, and Chanel. It bored me to tears, but the money was fabulous."

"What happened to her?" Samantha tilted her head, then blushed. "I'm sorry, that's none of my..."

"She had an affair with a man, got pregnant, then married him." I sighed. "They've been together now for twelve years, and though it pains me to say this, she's far happier with Pierre than she ever was with me."

Samantha's mouth dropped open. "That's horrible!"

"It was a long time ago," I said, trying to brush it off. "But that experience taught me to never forget the importance of love and loyalty in any relationship. I don't mean to sound too philosophical, but it's true."

Samantha nodded, her cheeks still bright red. After a few moments of awkward silence, she cleared her throat.

"So, what happened after Juliette?" She asked. "It sounds like you didn't stay in Paris for very long."

I shook my head. "No, I left France shortly after she married Pierre. I went back to Bucharest and started auditioning for more television shows and movies. I had some success over the next few years, but when I returned to New York, my career took off. And now I'm here, pretending to be a movie star."

"Babies are career killers in Hollywood." Samantha traced the rim of her glass with her index finger. "I've sometimes wondered if... never mind."

"Wondered what?" I suspected she was hiding something. "Do you have baby fever like most of my straight girlfriends?"

Samantha's hand shot out, and her drink spilled all over the table. "Oh my God, I'm so sorry." She grabbed a few paper napkins out of the dispenser on the side of the table and began mopping up the mess.

"It's okay," I breathed. Samantha might not realize it, but she wore her heart on her sleeve. I'd said something to startle her, but I felt uncomfortable digging any deeper. We'd only just reconnected, and I didn't want to frighten her off.

"Samantha, you haven't even been drinking and you're making a mess." The waitress laughed and finished cleaning the table. "Do you want another Mango Tango?"

"Yes, but this time with rum." Samantha rubbed her temples and grimaced. "I told myself I'd stop drinking, but I'm not about to listen to a quitter."

Chapter Eight
Morgan

"... hen his personal assistant strolled in and started recording Brock singing karaoke." Samantha was telling me hysterical stories about movie stars she knew. "But neither of them realized he wasn't just recording Brock making a fool of himself. He'd accidentally started a live stream. Brock started dancing like he was a Rockette on Broadway, and his voice was horrifically off key. By the following morning, the video went viral. That poor kid never got another PA job in Hollywood."

"Oh my God, remind me never to have a personal assistant." I giggled. "I know that's supposed to be a perk of the job, but I'd feel so uncomfortable having someone following me around. Maybe I'm not cut out for the Hollywood lifestyle."

Samantha smiled and took a sip of her drink. "You never know. If this movie is a hit, you'll need one. You just have to be sure to set boundaries and treat them well. It's always the stars who act like total divas that get screwed over by their assistants."

I wasn't sure how I felt about potentially hiring someone to help me with tasks in my life, but I knew Samantha was right. I'd seen actors on TV or in movies treating their personal assistants like shit, and it didn't seem like a good idea.

"All right," I said with a sigh, "we'll see what happens when (or if) this movie takes off." We both laughed and clinked our glasses together before finishing our drinks.

It felt so comfortable being with her, almost like we'd never stopped being friends. Maybe it was the booze, or maybe the attraction we used to feel for each other never went away. We'd been sitting in this booth for hours now, telling one funny story after another. Thank God I didn't have to work tomorrow, and I hoped Samantha didn't have an early morning.

"Ladies, gather 'round because DJ Femme Fatale is in the house, and we're about to set this place on fire! I'm here to ignite your night with beats that'll move your soul and rhythms that'll make your heart race. So, grab your best dancing partner or strut out there solo, because it's time to unleash your inner dance diva." Beats began to thump through the speakers. "Let's create a sonic journey together that celebrates love, life, and the incredible energy in this room. Get ready to groove, let loose, and feel the music deep within your bones. Are you with me, party people? Let's do this!"

Most of the women clapped, and several couples got on the dance floor.

"Remember junior prom?" Without thinking, I reached across the table and took Samantha's hand. "You were with that awful Billy, and I can't even remember the loser I was with."

Samantha looked into my eyes and gave me a slow smile. "It was Tyler, if I remember correctly."

I laughed and shook my head. "Of course you do." I paused for a moment, gathering my courage before continuing. "What I never told you back then was that all night long, I really wanted to dance with you. But I knew everyone would freak out if we did, so I just stayed away."

Samantha squeezed my hand tightly as she stared into my eyes. She seemed lost in her own thoughts before finally speaking again. "We could have found some way to sneak away," she said wistfully.

The musical beats emanating from the speakers grew louder as the DJ began to mix up the crowd on the dance floor. The music thumped around us like a constant reminder of what could have been between us. If only life had gone differently all those years ago.

"Come on," Samantha said suddenly, standing up and pulling me to my feet with her free hand. "Let's dance!"

Before I could protest or think of any excuses not to go out there, we were threading our way through the crowd towards the center of the room.

Once there, Samantha's grip around me tightened, her fingers digging into the small of my back. Her body was pressed snug against mine and I could feel every curve of her figure molding perfectly with my own. I felt a stirring down below as her thigh brushed teasingly against mine.

"Junior prom would've been much better if we'd been with each other." Samantha murmured in my ear, her voice a sultry purr that sent shivers down my spine. My breath hitched as the memory flashed in my mind- awkward dancing, stolen glances and longing looks from across the room.

She pulled away slightly, allowing me to look into her sparkling eyes, which were brimming with unspoken emotions. Making up for lost time, our lips crashed together, tongues tangling and exploring each other fervently. She tasted sinfully sweet - like mangos and rum - a combination that left me craving more.

My hands moved lower, cupping her firm ass and pulling her even closer against me. She gasped, and I took the opportunity to delve deeper into her mouth, making her moan. She ran her fingers through my hair, tugging gently when I nipped at her plump bottom lip. Our bodies continued to move rhythmically to the thumping music that filled the air around us while we lost ourselves in each other.

Breaking apart for air, I trailed wet kisses along her neck. Her soft whimpers spurred me on further, making me want to explore more of the goddess trapped in my arms.

"Dance floor is too public," she purred against my ear before taking it between her teeth lightly. "Time for a private dance." With that cryptic statement, she took hold of my hand, dragging me off the pulsating dance floor towards what looked like a secluded part of the club.

Once we were out of prying eyes, she pushed me onto a plush sofa before straddling my lap. She ran her hands through her tousled hair, while I gripped her luscious hips to steady myself.

With one swift move, I flipped our positions and now I loomed over her, my eyes drinking in every inch of her intoxicating body.

"Fuck," she groaned breathlessly, bucking up against me. Then suddenly, she froze.

"Babe, what's happening?"

"That woman standing in the corner over there," Samantha nodded her head. "She's my boss's ex-girlfriend, and from what I understand, she's trouble."

I subtly shifted my gaze and saw a stunning woman with short black hair and alabaster skin wearing jeans and a scuffed leather jacket.

"Her name is Jody, and she's..."

The woman abruptly left.

"Who cares about her?" I nuzzled Samantha's neck and was rewarded with a groan. "I've only got eyes for you. Kiss me again."

My lips crashed against Samantha's, and I felt her surrender. Fervent heat ran through my veins as I deepened the kiss, exploring every inch of her mouth as if it were the most precious thing in the world.

Samantha's hands tangled in my hair as she pulled me closer, and I eagerly obliged. I had never felt so alive before; her scent intoxicated me and the feel of her skin against mine was pure bliss.

I trailed wet kisses along her neck, relishing each moan that escaped from her lips. Her hips shifted up towards me with a seductive rhythm that was driving me wild.

As our bodies moved together, all thoughts of Jody left my mind until there was only Samantha and I. Nothing else mattered at this moment but us—the music that swelled around us, the heat radiating off our bodies and the undeniable electricity that seemed to be binding us together like glue.

Finally breaking apart for air, we both lay breathless on the sofa.

"Who cares about anybody but us?" I chuckled lightly before nuzzling into Samantha's neck. She giggled softly before running her fingers through my hair and pressing gentle kisses onto my forehead and cheeks.

"You're right," she smiled softly before pecking me on the lips one last time. "I've only got eyes for you."

"I need more," I breathed. "We have too many clothes on, and I'm not prepared to put on a show for the crowd."

My words jarred us back to reality. There were easily a hundred woman dancing around us, and I'd never been an exhibitionist.

"Will you come home with me?" Samantha purred.

Chapter Nine
Samantha

"I thought you'd never ask." Morgan stroked my cheek. Then she pulled me to my feet and started dragging me through the crowd toward the exit.

The club was a blaze of noise, heaving bodies, and strobe lights. I felt dizzy with anticipation as I followed Morgan through it. The other women were watching us as we made our way through the throng.

As we neared the exit, Morgan grabbed my hand, our fingers interlocking, and I felt her body trembling. I looked up into her eyes, and she said, "My first time should've been with you, Samantha."

People were getting out of our way, their eyes widening as if they knew what we were about to do. A wild energy coursed between us, and all I wanted was to make love with her.

In what seemed like a blur, we were standing outside on the street, the chill night air causing us to pause for a moment.

"Let's go to your place," Morgan whispered. Without hesitation, I nodded. We started walking quickly, almost running, as if we were being chased. When we got to my car, I opened the doors and as soon as we were seated, I reached over to Morgan and pulled her into my arms for another kiss.

Morgan's heart pounded against mine as we explored each other's mouths. I wanted her so badly, and it felt like everything else had melted away.

Suddenly, there was a loud knock on my window. Startled, I pulled away from Morgan and looked up to see a police officer standing outside the car.

"Oh shit," I mumbled, and lowered my window.

"Hey," he said, "you two should get a room if you want to do that kind of thing."

My cheeks flushed. "Yes, sir," I stammered, my voice shaking slightly.

"Have a um, fun night ladies." He strolled off, and Morgan and I exchanged embarrassed looks before bursting out laughing. When we finally calmed down, I brushed my lips over hers and sighed.

"Let's hurry." I rolled up the window and started the engine. "We've got a lot of catching up to do."

* * *

As we approached the door to my apartment, I felt a giddy mix of anticipation and excitement. Morgan gripped my hand in hers as I opened the door and stepped inside.

The soft light of the streetlights outside the windows illuminated the stylish interior. Everything sparkled and glowed, and I felt Morgan's eyes on me as we gazed at each other in wonder.

Before I could take another breath, Morgan spun me

around and pressed me against the wall, her lips meeting mine with an intensity that made my pussy clench. Her hands roamed my body hungrily, sending shivers through me with every touch.

I melted into her embrace as we kissed, our mouths exploring each other's hungrily. The chemistry between us was undeniable; it felt like no time had passed since we were last together, though we were now going to finally make love. Every fiber of my being ached for her, and suddenly, all I wanted was to get lost in her embrace forever.

"I need you in my bed, now," I gasped, then took Morgan's hand and dragged her down the hallway. When we got to the door, I eyed Morgan and licked my lips. "Finally, we get to really make love."

"I'm kind of glad we waited," Morgan breathed. "Teenagers don't know what they're doing, and I'm going to make you come so hard you see stars."

I pushed open the bedroom door, and for a split second felt oddly shy. When we were kids, we'd spent many nights together. But we'd never gone further than kissing and touching each other on top of our clothes. But now Morgan would see me naked for the first time.

"I've waited so long for this," Morgan's gaze dropped do my feet and slowly crept back up to my face.

I backed away from her, feeling a mixture of apprehension and excitement. There was no turning back now; I was ready to give myself to her completely and indulge in the pleasure we'd spent years longing for.

Bracing myself against the wall, Morgan's body molded to mine. Then slowly, ever so slowly, her lips feathered over mine. My mouth opened, and her tongue glided across my lower lip. I felt a surge of desire when she touched me, and her hand eagerly traced my breasts through my bra.

"I need you naked," she whispered huskily into my ear before seizing my bottom lip between hers, sucking softly. Her fingers made swift work of unbuttoning my blouse, and she let it fall to the floor.

She released my mouth to trail fervent kisses down the column of my neck, her fingers fumbling to get my bra off. The air was cool against my exposed flesh as she pulled back to admire what she'd uncovered. "You're so beautiful," she murmured, her gaze raking over me.

My breath hitched as she delicately traced the pad of her thumb around one nipple, causing it to tighten instantly in response. A moan tumbled from my lips as she leaned down to take it into her mouth, alternating between gentle suckling and teasing flicks of her tongue. My back arched reflexively off the wall at the raw pleasure spiking through me.

"You taste so good," she growled against my skin before moving her attention to the other aroused tip. She rewarded my gasp with a smirk against my skin.

"Morgan... I need more..." I pleaded breathlessly, running my hands desperately through her hair. "I must see you. Please, take your clothes off."

Guiding me towards the bed, she pushed me on it. I watched, transfixed, as Morgan undressed. She moved with a tantalizingly slow sway of her hips, and as each article of clothing came off, she'd let it fall to the ground. Finally, she stood before me in nothing but a pair of sheer white panties.

My breath caught in my throat at the sight of her; I couldn't help but admire how perfect she looked. Her skin glowed like velvet in the soft light filtering in through the window, and I could feel my desire for her growing with every passing second.

"Look at me," Morgan demanded, her voice dripping with desire. I was breathless as our eyes locked. A primal need ignited between us that we'd held at bay for far too long.

Slowly, she directed my hands to the waistband of her sheer white panties—the last barrier to seeing all of her— letting them rest there momentarily before guiding them down over the gentle swell of her hips. Our fingers tangled together in their shared task, both sets trembling with anticipation.

The fabric slid off her long legs and pooled on the floor at her feet. My eyes traced every curve and valley, my body reacting instinctively, as if it had been waiting for this moment all along.

"Morgan," I breathed, unable to keep the whimper from escaping my lips. A wicked smile played on hers as she crawled onto the bed toward me.

My hands roamed across her skin freely now, tracing the indentations of her ribs and the swell of her breasts before cupping them gently. The slight bounce sent a wave of heat through me.

Her nipples hardened into pebbled nubs against my palm —the texture was intoxicating and caused an inexplicable pull deep within me. Leaning down, I lavished each breast with attention, licking around their hardened peaks in slow tantalizing circles before taking one between my teeth gently. Her gasp echoed in my ears alongside the pulsing arousal coursing through my veins.

"Mmm," she moaned lowly, arching into me as pleasure consumed her senses. "Touch me... I want you inside."

A sense of urgency took over as our bodies heated up

under each other's touch. My hands ventured lower, trailing along the smooth plain of her stomach, only stopping when they reached the juncture between her thighs.

She was wet; her arousal coating my fingers as they parted the lips of her sex. I relished in the feel of her, slick and inviting against my digits, begging to be filled.

I slid one finger, then another inside her with practiced ease, drawing a shiver that rippled across her body. She clenched around me—tight and warm—and I moved them in tandem with the rise and fall of her chest.

"I must taste you," I panted, my desire burning hot inside of me. Withdrawing my fingers, I slid down her body until my face hovered over her wet pussy. She trembled beneath me, anticipation radiating off of her in waves. Taking a deep breath, I lowered my head and pressed my lips against her sensitive folds.

The sweet essence of her filled me immediately, its richness almost overwhelming in its intensity. I began to lick and suck gently at her clitoris, circling it with delicate strokes as she moaned and writhed beneath me in ecstasy. Her hips rocked in time with my movements as she reached higher and higher levels of pleasure.

My tongue traveled lower now, exploring every inch of her until I reached the entrance to her tight sheath. Slipping past the barrier, I delved deeper into her depths, slipping one finger then another inside as my tongue caressed the inner walls of her channel. My thumb brushed against the sensitive bundle of nerves at the top of her sex and Morgan grabbed the sides of my head, holding me in place.

Her moans grew louder and more urgent as I continued to pleasure her, my fingers and tongue working in perfect harmony to drive her closer and closer to the edge. She was so close now, I could feel it in the way her body quivered beneath me, her hips thrusting up to meet my touch.

"S-Samantha," she gasped out, her voice a plea as her fingers gripped my hair.

I answered with increased vigor—sinking both of my fingers into her slick depths and pressing hard against that bundle of nerves at the top—sliding my tongue against each inner wall until I felt her body lock up tight beneath me.

"Yes," she cried out, a wave of pleasure washing over us both as she shuddered through a powerful orgasm. I kept going until every last wave had dissipated, drinking in the sight of Morgan in such a state of bliss.

Finally, when she was spent, I withdrew my hand from between her legs and kissed my way up her body; savoring each brush of my lips against her skin until our mouths met hungrily in a passionate kiss. When we broke apart, Morgan licked her lips. "Your turn, Samantha."

Morgan cupped my breast, then took my swollen nipple in her mouth. My back arched, and I made a sound I'd never made with any other woman before. It was animalistic, a deep groan that sounded like it came from the depths of my soul.

Morgan's lips moved from my breasts to my neck, trailing passionate kisses as her hands roamed over my body. She delicately circled my nipples with her fingertips before taking one of them into her mouth and sucking gently. I gasped at the sensation, a ripple of pleasure coursing through me as she swirled her tongue around the sensitive bud.

Her hand moved lower, tracing circles over my stomach before slipping between my legs. Two of her fingers expertly worked their way inside me as she massaged and caressed my inner walls with a gentle rhythm that had me arching towards her. The sensations were overwhelming, each thrust of her fingers sending shockwaves of pleasure throughout my body.

"You're so beautiful, Samantha," Morgan whispered. Then she kept exploring every inch of me until I was trembling with desire. Morgan seemed to sense this and pulled away, replacing her fingers with her tongue as she licked and sucked on my most sensitive areas. My hips bucked uncontrollably as I came undone beneath her touch, wave upon wave of pleasure crashing over me until I couldn't take anymore.

"Oh my God, where have you been all my life?" I breathed, then worried that I'd said too much. Scaring Morgan away was the last thing I wanted to do. But it was so rare to find someone so attuned to my body. It was as if she could read my mind, knowing exactly how and where to touch me to provoke such intense pleasure.

"Baby, I've been waiting for this moment," Morgan kissed the tip of my nose, then curled her body next to mine. "And now we have to make up for lost time."

Chapter Ten
Morgan

The morning sun was beaming through the window, casting a warm gold light across the room. I lazily opened my eyes, feeling the warmth of Samantha's body curled against me. We were both still nude from the night before, her skin a light gold compared to my own pale complexion. I ran my fingers gently over her bare arm and smiled, watching as her chest softly rose and fell with her breath.

In the stillness of the morning, I lay there for a time, savoring the moment. I felt truly content, and for the first time in a long while, I was happy. Being with Samantha felt so natural and effortless, as if no other person in the world mattered. I wanted to stay in this moment forever, yet I also craved more. I wanted to explore these feelings further, to discover what else might be hidden beneath.

Suddenly, Samantha stirred. "Good morning," she murmured, her voice husky with sleep.

"Good morning," I replied, smiling down at her. I leaned

in and brushed my lips across hers. "You are so beautiful. It's almost unreal."

My words hung in the air between us, and I felt a warmth spread through my chest as I watched her reaction. She smiled softly and averted her gaze, but not before I saw the blush rise to her cheeks.

"I can't believe you're here in my bed," she murmured, still looking away from me.

"Neither can I," I replied, resting my hand on her arm. We lay there for a moment in comfortable silence, simply enjoying being together. The night before had been magical - full of laughter and passionate lovemaking - and yet now that morning had come, I felt more wary. Words of emotion lingered unspoken on our lips, as if neither of us wanted to say too much too soon.

Finally, Samantha rolled onto her side and met my gaze with an affectionate smile. "Do you want to go get breakfast?" she asked, breaking the silence between us.

"I'd love to, but I have a full day." I said and felt a tiny pang of regret at the little lie I just told her. What I needed was a little space to process my emotions. "I'd love it if my realtor could start the paperwork for the condo. Living in a hotel sucks."

A slow smile spread across Samantha's cheeks. "I'll get to it first thing. Also, I'll reach out to the seller and see if I can get her to lower the price a bit."

"You don't..."

"I'm your realtor. It's my job to get you the best deal possible." Samantha stroked my cheek. "Hopefully, I'll have a contract ready for you to sign by tomorrow. Since I can't interest you in breakfast, how about a little coffee before you leave?"

I ran my fingers along Samantha's bare arm, marveling at the smoothness of her skin. I couldn't help but give in to the temptation of exploring further. I caressed the curve of her neck before lightly tracing my fingers across her chest. My heart quickened as I felt her breath catch in anticipation.

Gently, I moved my hand lower and grazed my thumb over a hardened nipple. A soft moan escaped Samantha's lips as she arched into me, and I felt a rush of desire. With one last lingering touch, I pulled away and looked into her eyes.

"I'd rather spend a little more time in bed with you."

"Here we are." Samantha turned to me as we pulled up to my hotel. "I'm heading straight to the office. I might need to speak with you later today after I talk to the seller. Do you think we could have dinner together this evening?"

"I was just about to ask you the same thing." I leaned over and brushed my lips across her cheek. "Call me when you're done with work. Oh, but I can't stay out late like last night. Rehearsals start tomorrow."

As I stepped out of the car, I felt sadness wash over me. Saying goodbye to Samantha was difficult. In the space of a few hours, she'd once again become the center of my world. It was like we'd never been apart for all those years.

I stood there for a moment, watching as she drove away until she was just a tiny dot in the distance. Sighing, I turned towards the hotel lobby and walked inside. My mind raced with thoughts about Samantha and our relationship. It would be so easy to fall for her; her beauty, her intelligence, her, well, everything. But then again, why should I risk it?

I'd just moved to Hollywood and had so much going on. The movie was going into rehearsals, and I was about to be the proud owner of an actual penthouse. Not in my wildest dreams did I ever think this would be possible. But an actual relationship? That wasn't part of my plan. But then again, reuniting with Samantha was a once in a lifetime occurrence. Did I really want to spend the rest of my life regretting not pursuing a relationship with her?

I headed toward a row of elevators, but when I passed the restaurant in the lobby, my stomach growled. Since I hadn't eaten since yesterday, I decided to grab a bite before heading upstairs.

I stepped into The Rosewood Tea Room, the smell of freshly brewed tea and warm scones filling the air. As I looked around, I admired the elegant decor, with velvet chairs and carved wooden tables.

"Good morning, right this way please," the hostess greeted me with a radiant smile. "Here is your table. Let me know if there's anything I can get for you. What can I get you to drink?"

"A cup of English Breakfast tea would really hit the spot."

The server left, and moments later, she returned and poured a cup of tea for me, the warm steam enveloping my face. "I'll be back to take your order in a couple of minutes."

My eyes widened as they scanned over all the delicious sounding dishes. The menu included egg salad and roasted vegetable sandwiches, raspberry jam scones, and cream cheese pastries. Everything looked so good that I wanted to order a little of everything. But I'm sure the wardrobe department wouldn't be pleased with that.

The server returned to my table and smiled warmly at me. "What can I get for you?"

I looked over the menu again, trying to decide what I wanted. Finally, I settled on the sandwich with egg salad and roasted vegetables, as well as a scone with raspberry jam. "I'll have the sandwich and scone please," I said.

"Excellent choice," she said, jotting down my order on her notepad. "Would you like anything else?"

"No, thanks."

She nodded and wrote something down before leaving to place my order. Moments later, she returned with my order on a tray. She carefully placed it in front of me, along with another cup of steaming English Breakfast tea and some clotted cream for my scone.

The food was out of this world, but now I regretted not eating with Samantha. But I had to admit, making love with her again this morning was worth it.

There was something so special about her, though there were still some mysteries to be solved. From what she'd said, there was a lot of stress in her life. Samantha's real estate business had apparently suffered, and hopefully it would pick up now that she'd sold me the penthouse. I suspected there was something else, something deeper, that troubled her. If I had to lay money on it, I bet it had something to do with her past.

"Our past," I murmured aloud, then downed the last of my tea.

"Will there be anything else?" The server was pretty, a California blonde who was probably an out of work actress.

"No, thanks." I dabbed at my lips with a napkin. "Charge it to my room, thanks."

As I walked back out into the lobby, a familiar face caught my eye. It was the same woman that Samantha had pointed out to me last night at the lesbian bar. She was dressed in black leather from head to toe and had an air of danger about her. Her dark hair was pulled back in a sleek ponytail, and she wore motorcycle boots and a jacket with flames on the back.

She didn't seem to fit in amongst the other guests in the hotel lobby, and yet she held her head high with an air of confidence that couldn't be denied. Our eyes met briefly. Then she strolled up to the front desk. Curiosity got the best of me, so I followed behind her. When I got to the desk, I smiled at a clerk and made up a reason for me to be there.

"Hello, I'm in room 620. Do I have any messages?"

"Good morning, Ms. Sterling." The clerk was an older man wearing a charcoal gray suit. "It looks like you have several of them. Let me print them out for you. It will only be a moment." The man typed into his computer. "There's two from a man named Rob Harrison, and several more from Eva Thorne." The man's eyes widened. Everyone in LA knew who Eva was. While he continued to type, I did my best to listen to what the strange woman in black leather was saying.

The woman leaned against the hotel's front desk, her leather jacket adorned with patches and her expression determined. With a sly grin, she leaned in close to the hotel clerk.

"Hey there, sweetheart," Jody purred, her smoky voice dripping with charisma. "I'm looking for Declan Montgomery, you know, the handsome fella who's been gracing your fancy establishment? I heard he's been seen around here."

The hotel clerk, a bit flustered by her bold approach,

glanced around nervously. "I'm sorry, ma'am, I can't just give out guest information."

She raised an arched eyebrow and slipped a business card onto the counter. "Listen, darlin', I'm not looking to cause any trouble. I just need to give him a package." Her fingers lightly tapped the card, suggesting a discreet note or invitation. "Can you help a girl out?" She winked.

My curiosity was piqued as I watched the scene unfold. The woman in black leather had certainly caught my attention, but now I was dying to know what she wanted with Declan Montgomery. Who was this dangerous-looking but beautiful woman trying to get the room number of a famous movie star?

The clerk was noticeably flustered. "You may leave a package with me," he said, his face turning red. "I'll be sure to give it to Mr. Montgomery."

"No can do," the woman frowned. "I'm telling ya, Declan's going to be pissed off about this. Tell him Jody stopped by, and also tell him how you wouldn't let me in." The woman gave him a dazzling smile and thanked him before turning away from the desk and striding past me out of the lobby. I watched her go, my mind racing with questions: who was this mysterious woman? Samantha mentioned something about her boss and this woman, and that they used to date. Apparently, Samantha's boss had a thing for criminals. At least it appeared like the woman was sketchy. When I saw Samantha later tonight, I'd mention it to her.

"Ma'am?" the clerk said, and I jumped.

"I'm so sorry, I lost my train of thought." I shrugged. "Can I have my messages, please?"

The man laid a small stack of papers in front of me.

Glancing through them, I saw that most of them were either from Eva, the film's director, or the studio. A couple of them were from my agent, so I'd give him a call as soon as I got to my room.

"Thank you, sir." I spun around and headed for the elevator. I punched the up button, and a moment later, the doors opened. When I stepped inside, the doors began to shut, then an arm thrust through the closing doors. A moment later, the mysterious woman in leather stepped inside and eyed me.

"Going up?"

Chapter Eleven
Samantha

"Jesus, how did I get so lucky?" I murmured, then drove away from Morgan's hotel. Last night and this morning were perfect, and I was determined to ride this high for as long as I could.

"Let's listen to some music."

I switched on the radio. A soft, slow melody played, a familiar one that I'd heard before. It was a love song, one that always filled me with hope.

I sang along, my voice joining with the music in harmony.

In a crowded room, I caught your eye,
A lightning bolt, sparks started to fly.
You're not the one to play it coy,
We danced that night, just like a joyride, oh boy.

"Who the hell sings this?" I shook my head, then turned onto the exit ramp.

You're a little trouble, and I like the thrill,
In the midnight hour, you give me chills.
A love so wild, it's a burning flame,

We're playing with fire, but we're both to blame.
A car horn blared. "Shit, I cut that guy off. Sorry!"
It's not a fairy tale, no, it's not that neat,
Our love's a rollercoaster, can't be beat.
We're in too deep, can't hit the brakes,
This love's a storm. We'll do whatever it takes.

I switched off the radio because traffic was even more insane than usual. There was a special place in hell for the people who designed the San Diego Freeway.

"I'm not letting anything bother me today." I took a deep breath, then I saw a line of cars up ahead. In my lane. Not moving an inch. After I slowed down to a stop, I grabbed my phone out of my purse and typed a message to Gray.

> Stuck on the 405. I'll be at work ASAP.
> Morgan Sterling is buying the penthouse!

* * *

"Sorry I'm late, but traffic was hell."

Gray smiled and handed me a stack of folders. "You finally made a sale. I hope this means your string of bad luck is at an end." Gray leaned over his desk and whispered. "These folders are new listings, and I'm giving you first dibs. Sneak those into your office and don't let anyone know you got to see them first."

"Thanks," I winked. I turned to go to my office, and Gray giggled.

"Is that what I think it is?"

I turned back to him. "What are you talking about?"

Gray stood up and came around his desk. "You have a hickey under your left ear," he whispered.

I placed my hand over the spot and felt myself blush. "At least I'm getting some."

"Do you have any concealer?" He asked. "If not, I've got a tube, and we're about the same skin tone."

"Yes, of course I do." I shrugged. "Is the boss lady here?"

"No, it's your lucky day. Almost everyone is out of the office." Gray crossed his arms over his chest. "So tell me, who's the lucky woman?"

I wasn't in the mood to gossip about Morgan just yet, so I deflected.

"Me."

I raced down the hallway before he could stop me. When I got to my office, I shut the door and placed the folders on the corner of my desk. Gray was such a gossip, but he always had my back. Hopefully, I'd find a gem amongst the new listings and be able to sell them quickly.

After settling in, I leaned back in my chair with a satisfied smile on my face. I'd finally sold the penthouse to Morgan, and it felt like an enormous weight had been lifted off of my shoulders. As I reflected on last night, I could still feel myself blushing. No one had ever made me feel so special before. Even when we were teenagers, Morgan always knew how to put a smile on my face.

"Let's find another property to sell." I grabbed the folders off the corner of my desk and got to work.

* * *

"Samantha, could you come to my desk, please?" Gray's voice startled me.

I pushed the button on the intercom and replied, "Is it important? Because I'm very busy."

"The postal worker needs you to sign for a piece of certified mail."

Damn it.

"I'll be right there." I pushed my chair back and got to my feet. The paperwork for Morgan's closing was almost done, and I wanted to get it off my plate. Moments later, I strolled up to the reception area and saw a large woman with a clipboard in hand.

"I need you to sign here." The woman handed me a pen and the clipboard. After signing, she handed me a brown envelope.

As I stared down at it, I felt my stomach drop. The sender was the Mississippi Family Connection Bureau. My heart raced and my palms became sweaty.

I looked up and saw Gray standing there with a quizzical expression on his face. He knew something was wrong, but I wasn't ready to tell him yet.

"Is everything okay?" He asked cautiously.

I forced a smile onto my face and brushed past him without saying a word. I had to get back to my office before he could see the panic in my eyes.

As soon as the door shut behind me, I dropped the envelope onto my desk and sank into my chair. The name Mississippi Family Connection Bureau brought back memories I'd been trying to put behind me for years.

"Please, Jesus, don't let this be what I think it is."

Gathering up all of my courage, I took a deep breath and opened my top desk drawer and pulled out a letter opener.

"This is supposed to be a good day," I groaned, then heard feet racing down the hallway. Throwing the envelope in my desk, I forced a smile on my face.

"Samantha, you look like you saw a ghost." He sat down across from me. "What's going on? First you come into work like you're walking on sunshine, and now you get some mystery mail that clearly freaks you out. Tell me what's going on, and maybe I can help."

A tear slid down the side of my nose, and I swiped it away. "Gray, I can't talk about it."

"Can't talk about what?"

Charlotte stood in the doorway, frowning. "Gray, why are you here and not at your desk?"

Gray stood. "Sorry, Charlotte. I wasn't expecting you today. How did it go with your client?"

"The Vice-President in charge of programming for the StarView network is in reception, wondering if anyone can help her." Charlotte crossed her arms over her chest and scowled. "Get to work, Gray."

He raced past her. Then Charlotte shut the door and sat across from me.

"We need to talk," Charlotte murmured. Could this day get any worse?

"I haven't written you a paycheck in five months," she began, and I felt sweat dripping down my sides. "And a friend of Julianna's saw you at a bar last night partying your ass off with a beautiful woman. If you're not willing to put in the effort to sell properties, I'm stuck with no other option than to let you go."

I'd been dreading this day for weeks, but thankfully, I had good news for my boss.

"Actually, the woman I was with last night decided to purchase a penthouse." I shoved the paperwork for the closing across my desk. "Here's the paperwork."

A smile stretched across Charlotte's face. She glanced over the papers and murmured, "Not bad. Five million definitely puts you back in my good graces."

"Do you often have spies stalking me?" The words slipped out of my mouth before I could stop them. "What I do in my own time is nobody's business."

Charlotte sighed. "Samantha, you went from being my top producer to being my lowest over the last few months, and I'm worried about you. Half the time you drag yourself in here looking like you haven't slept, and of course I'm going to wonder what's going on. You can talk to me, Samantha. I'm more than your boss. I'm your friend."

She was also my ex. It had been a brief fling, and neither of us had let it affect our working together. What worried me the most was that she was literally seconds away from firing my ass. Why had l allowed my personal problems to interfere with my job? Charlotte had every right to expect more from me, and I'd disappointed her.

"I'm sorry, Charlotte," I began, my voice shaking slightly. "I won't let it happen again."

Charlotte nodded slowly, but there was still an underlying worry in her eyes. "It's okay, Samantha," she breathed. "Just... make sure you take some time for yourself, too. You need to look after yourself before you can look after others."

That was something I could do easily enough; staying up

late and partying wasn't how I wanted to spend my nights anymore anyway- not since reconnecting with Morgan.

"Okay," I replied softly, doing my best to swallow back the tears stinging my eyes. "Thank you."

Charlotte smiled at me sympathetically, then stood up, came around my desk, and patted me on the shoulder. "You're going to be fine," she said before leaving me alone with my thoughts.

When the door shut, I slapped the top of my desk. "Fuck, that hurt!" I grabbed a tissue out of my purse and dabbed at my eyes. This day had started out so wonderfully, and now it was just one gut punch after another.

"Get yourself together, girl," I breathed.

I took a deep breath and slowly let it out, willing myself to calm down. This day had started off so good - reconnecting with Morgan and selling that penthouse - and I couldn't let it end on a sour note.

First things first, I needed to get my personal life in order. I needed to see how things panned out with Morgan. After losing her all those years ago, we deserved another chance.

Second, I had to focus on my career. Thanks to the five million dollar sale, Charlotte seemed satisfied for now. But I didn't want to become complacent with just one sale. I knew there were more opportunities if I pushed myself and aimed higher.

Finally, I had to remember that taking care of myself was just as important as anything else. Life could be hectic sometimes, but it was important that I took breaks when I needed them and gave myself the time necessary for self-care. As long as I kept all these things in mind, then surely everything would work out alright in the end?

"But what the hell am I going to do about this?" I pulled the certified letter out of my desk and stared at it. If it was like the other letters I'd gotten from the Mississippi Family Connection Bureau, I had a massive decision to make. With trembling hands, I opened the brown envelope.

Chapter Twelve
Morgan

The doors closed and the elevator jolted upwards, our reflections flickering in the mirrored walls. The space between us felt charged with electricity, as though we were two opposing magnets drawn together in this tiny box.

I couldn't help stealing glances at her, trying to decipher the enigma that was this woman. With each passing second, my curiosity grew stronger until it overpowered me. "Excuse me," I said, hoping to engage her in conversation. "I heard you say at the front desk that you wanted to see Declan Montgomery. He's the movie star, right?"

She turned to me with a knowing smile, and I knew then that I was treading on dangerous ground.

"Normally, I'd tell you to mind your own fucking business." She stepped forward into my space. "But you're too beautiful. There's no way I'd want to hurt that face."

My heart was pounding. I'd never been flirted with like this before, and it felt strange and exciting. The stranger's eyes twinkled with mischief, as though she knew exactly what kind of game we were playing.

I suddenly found myself wanting to know more about her. Who was she? What was in the package she was delivering to the movie star?

The stranger must have sensed my apprehension because she reached out a hand and touched my arm. "It's alright," she said softly. "No harm done." Her voice was soothing and gentle, but there was an air of danger about her that made me feel both attracted and scared at the same time. Though I'd seen her at the gay bar last night, I decided to ask her a stupid question to see if she'd take the bait.

"So are you dating Declan or something?" I asked hesitantly. She chuckled softly and shook her head, her dark hair falling across her face in a tantalizing way that made me want to reach out and touch it.

"Wrong church, pretty lady," she replied, her voice taking on a mysterious quality that only served to increase my curiosity. "I'm here for business." She stepped back slightly, her lips curling into a sly smile that made me wonder just what kind of business this woman had in mind. "But if you're interested in finding out more about me..."

She trailed off suggestively, her eyes telling me everything without saying a word. I blushed furiously and looked away, embarrassed by my own boldness yet strangely exhilarated by the way the conversation had progressed so far.

The elevator doors opened on my floor. "Um, this is where I get off."

"You'd have a better time if I got you off." The woman bit her lower lip, and instead of being turned on by this stunning woman, I felt repulsed. Without another word I stepped off the elevator. When the doors shut, I leaned against the wall and shuddered. If I remembered right, her name was Jody something. I'd have to tell Samantha about running into her over dinner tonight.

When I got to my room, I searched for the key card in my purse. "Damn it, where the hell is the thing?" Finally, I found it, and let myself in.

When I'd left the restaurant I felt a little tired from eating too much. But after my encounter with that woman on the elevator, I was too wired to think of much else.

"The messages," I murmured, then pulled them out of my bag. After reading them, I decided to call my director first. Though we'd already met, the woman still made me nervous.

My stomach twisted into knots as I dialed the number Eva Thorne had given me. As the phone rang, I could feel my heart pounding in my chest. "This is Morgan Sterling returning your call," I said, struggling to keep my voice steady.

"Morgan!" Eva's voice came through loud and clear on the other end of the line. "I'm so glad you called. I have some script changes for you and wanted to run them by you before rehearsal tomorrow."

"Oh, great!" I exclaimed, trying to hide my nervousness. "What kind of changes?"

"Mostly dialogue," she said crisply. "I emailed you a copy with all the changes marked up, so if you could take some time tonight to read it over that would be great."

"Will do!" I replied cheerfully. "I can't wait for rehearsals tomorrow."

"Gotta go, Morgan. I have a meeting with wardrobe. See you in the morning."

Once she hung up, I sank into my chair and grabbed my

laptop from its spot on the desk. Opening up her email, I scanned through all the highlighted and revised lines until it was all sinking in. My biggest fear is they would change too much of the original play. Hollywood was constantly tweaking screenplays, and I didn't want them to mess up the original core story. So far, it looked like the changes were warranted.

My character Elizabeth was a free spirited artist, and from what I could see, they were making her a bit more bohemian. That suited me just fine, because my director of the Broadway show had made her too conservative. Now Elizabeth was reminding me of the Susan Sarandon character in the movie *The Witches Of Eastwick*. Elizabeth was a woman who opened up like a flower when she meets her love interest, William.

My phone dinged, and I snatched it up. It was a message from Samantha.

> I miss you. Where do you want to eat tonight?

My heart raced when I heard a knock at my hotel room door.

I checked myself in the bathroom mirror, then rushed to open it.

I gazed into Samantha's cobalt blue eyes and flashed a mischievous smile. "Did you miss me?" I winked playfully. Her lips curved up into a smirk, and then she stepped forward and took my face in her hands.

"More than you'll ever know," Samantha murmured, then

she brushed her lips across mine. I pulled her in closer, and deepened the kiss, relishing the taste of her.

When we finally broke apart, she stepped inside my suite and I followed closely behind her, eager to pick up where we left off. She let out a low laugh as I wrapped my arms around her waist and nuzzled into the crook of her neck.

"Missed you so damn much," she murmured into my ear, sending shivers down my spine.

"I missed you too," I replied softly, planting light kisses along her jawline before pulling away from her slightly so that we were looking eye to eye. "I had the strangest encounter earlier."

Samantha took my hand and led me to the beige sofa. Hotel room beige, my least favorite color. After setting her purse down on the chrome and glass coffee table she said, "Tell me all about it."

We sat down, and Samantha kissed the palm of my hand.

"Do you remember pointing out that woman to me at the bar last night?" I shut my eyes for a moment, remembering our brief conversation in the elevator. "You said her name was Jody, I believe."

"Jody Agnew? Where did you see her?" Samantha's brows furrowed.

"In the lobby. She was at the front desk trying to get the room number of Declan Montgomery." I squeezed her hand. "Of course, they wouldn't give it to her. So she left. But when I got on the elevator to come to my room, she got on it with me."

"Declan Montgomery is a known cokehead." Samantha drawled. "Jody was probably delivering cocaine. But, who knows? I don't know her that well, except she and my boss have a history together."

"You know, the woman is very attractive, but at the same time she repulses me. Like there's something evil to the core buried inside of her." I remembered her touching my arm and shivered.

"Well, I'm glad you're repulsed by her." Samantha stroked my arm. "I'm not good at sharing."

Did Samantha just lay claim to me somehow? Even though we'd just reunited, the thought of her feeling possesive about me provoked a smile.

"What are you grinning about?" Samantha scooted a little closer and laid her hand on my thigh.

"Nothing, well, everything. Everything is happening so fast." I stood up and went to the bar on the other side of the room. I pulled two bottles of water out of the mini-fridge and held them up. "Want one?"

"Thanks."

I handed her the bottle and settled next to her. "I start rehearsals tomorrow morning, and I'm about to close on the most expensive property I've ever bought. And of course, reuniting with you is the best change possible. It all feels unreal somehow."

"Speaking of the closing, I'll have the paperwork ready for you in two days. Plus, I was able to lower the price by a few thousand." Samantha's eyes lit up. She obviously loved her work.

"Enough about me," I purred and placed my arm over her shoulders. "Anything exciting happen to you today?"

Samantha's eyes darkened, then she smiled. "I almost got fired today."

I couldn't believe what I was hearing. My Samantha, was about to be fired from her job?

"What did you do?" Her eyes were wide and filled with fear.

"Charlotte, my boss, said she was going to fire me because I haven't had a sale in months and she's been on my case."

Samantha glanced away, embarrassed. She obviously felt ashamed of her performance. "When I told her about you buying the penthouse, she decided to let me stay."

I breathed a sigh of relief when Samantha told me she wasn't going to be fired after all.

"That's a huge relief." I said, pulling her in closer. "I'm so sorry. For some reason I think of you as being the best at whatever you do. You're strong, and vibrant." I combed my fingers through the back of her hair. "And damned sexy."

Samantha sighed, and I sensed something else was wrong. "Thanks. I also got a letter from, oh, never mind. Let's just say that the only good parts of my day involved you. Everything else was just meh."

"Little old me?" I winked. "That's good to know. I know several ways to make it better." I squeezed her thigh, and the desire I saw in Samantha's eyes was unmistakeable. "So, how about we put the bad parts of the day behind us and focus on something more fun?"

Samantha returned my smile, her cheeks turning a deep shade of pink. "What did you have in mind?"

I drew her in close, feeling the swell of her breasts press against my chest as she sighed into me. Her scent was alluring, a mix of perfume and the faint hint of natural musk that drove me wild. We sat there on the couch, our bodies inching closer as the tension built between us.

"Didn't you mention a letter?" I asked, my voice low and husky with anticipation, as I traced lazy circles up her thigh.

"Trust me," Samantha murmured against my neck, "it's nothing interesting compared to you. Jesus, Morgan, you drive me wild." Her fingers grazed the length of my arm, igniting a trail of desire that settled deep in my gut.

Her words emboldened me and without further ado, I slid a hand along the curve of her hip, appreciating just how soft she was through the fabric of her pencil skirt. My thumb brushed against the band of her lacey thong peeping out from underneath her skirt; it was an invitation I couldn't refuse. "Are you sure?" I teased, letting my fingers wander under the elastic.

"Positive." She half-shuddered and bit down on her lip; her eyes darkening with desire. Suddenly all business-like pretenses were forgotten, replaced by raw animalistic need.

As my digits ventured further inside her warmth, Samantha gasped, throwing back her head to reveal a tantalizing expanse of creamy neck that begged for attention. I leaned forward to meet it with my lips while kneading her with measured strokes that left her squirming for more.

"Oh god," she moaned as I applied pressure exactly where she needed it most. The sexy whimpers escaping from those cherry red lips cranked up the heat in me tenfold.

Samantha shifted in response to my touch - an enticing dance beneath my fingertips. Damn, she was exquisite; a living work of art who fit perfectly in the cradle of my arms.

"I want you. All of you," I growled into her ear, staking my claim over this divine being writhing next to me.

"You've got me," She whispered against my lips before capturing them in a searing kiss. "All of me, Morgan. All of me."

Chapter Thirteen
Samantha

I felt the warmth of Morgan's body beside me, and as I opened my eyes, I could feel our time together slipping away. We'd spent the late afternoon and early evening together, making love and ordering room service, letting the hours pass us by.

The streetlights from outside illuminated the room, and I looked at Morgan's face, so peaceful in sleep. I knew that she had to be up early to go to rehearsals for her new movie, so I reluctantly disengaged myself from her.

I got up from the bed, and as I gathered my clothes, I did my best to move quietly, so as not to disturb Morgan's slumber. I took one last look at her, lying there in the bed, and I let out a deep sigh. I wished the night could last forever, but I knew that it was time to go.

So I dressed, then scribbled a note letting her know I'd left so she could get a full night sleep.

"Where are you going?" Morgan's sleepy voice rang out. I turned, went to the bed and kissed her forehead.

"What time are you due at the studio?"

"Six," Morgan sighed. "And I probably won't leave until after six. That's the only horrible thing about being an actor. The hours are horrible."

"You get some sleep, babe. We'll talk tomorrow after work." I kissed her again, then crept out of her room. As much as I wanted to spend the night with her, I had a lot on my mind, and needed some space to sort things out.

* * *

I opened the door to my apartment, and wanted nothing more than to curl up in bed and pass out. After kicking off my shoes and setting my purse down, I wanted nothing more than to pour myself a stiff drink but thought better of it.

Instead of booze, I opted for water. I grabbed a glass from the counter and turned, about to make my way to the couch when I stopped in my tracks. The room was dark, lit only by a soft glow coming from the hallway, and it felt almost peaceful.

I made my way over to the couch and sat down. In the darkness I was alone with my thoughts, and in that moment, nothing else seemed to matter.

I rubbed my aching feet, wishing I could've spent the night with Morgan. But I struggled to wake up in the morning, and didn't want to cause her to be late to rehearsals. She'd said something earlier about taking risks, and to be true to yourself. But how could I do that?

"Fuck it," I muttered, then turned on the lamp on the side table next to me. I needed to reread that letter and make a decision, but I dreaded it. This was possibly the hardest decision I'll ever make, and no matter what I decided, somebody would be hurt. I got up, grabbed my purse, then settled down again. The envelope shook in my hands as I opened it, then I forced myself to read it again.

Dear Miss Bishop,

Re: Notification of Contact Request from Biological Son

We hope this correspondence finds you well. We are writing to inform you of a matter of utmost importance. The Mississippi Family Connection Bureau, acting in accordance with applicable state and federal laws, has received a formal request from a party indicating their desire to establish contact with you, their biological mother.

After a thorough review of our records, it has come to our attention that you made the selfless and challenging decision to place your child for adoption approximately twenty-one years ago. The individual in question, whose identity and information will remain confidential until such time as you choose to proceed, has expressed a heartfelt desire to initiate contact with you.

In accordance with the Mississippi Adoption Records Confidentiality Act, we must inform you of your rights and options regarding this request:

• **Right to Privacy**: You have the unassailable right to maintain your privacy and may decline any contact with the requesting party without further obligation.

• **Right to Consent**: If you are open to the possibility of contact, you may grant your consent for communication to proceed. In this event, the Bureau will facilitate communication while ensuring confidentiality is maintained.

. . .

• **Mediated Contact**: Should you wish, the Bureau is prepared to assist in mediating the initial contact, ensuring it transpires in a supportive and controlled manner.

It is crucial to emphasize that your rights and preferences are of paramount importance in this matter. No decision is required at this stage, and you may take as much time as necessary to consider the situation and make an informed choice. Your decision will be honored without reservation.

In the coming weeks, our Bureau will be in contact with you to discuss your wishes and provide additional information regarding your available options. In the interim, if you have any inquiries or concerns, please do not hesitate to reach out to our office.

Your understanding and cooperation are deeply appreciated as we navigate this sensitive matter together. We understand the significance of this communication and are committed to ensuring your rights and emotions are safeguarded throughout the process.

Thank you for your attention to this correspondence. We look forward to assisting you in any way that you deem fit.

Yours sincerely,

Melanie Brown

Melanie Brown

Social Worker

As I read those words again, the weight of their **significance** pressed down on me like a boulder. The room seemed to close in, and I felt the prickling of tears behind my eyelids. The past, which I had buried so deep within myself, was clawing its way to the surface, unearthing emotions I thought were long healed.

I'd given up my child for adoption over two decades ago, a decision made in a whirlwind of anguish and desperation. That chapter of my life had been carefully sealed away, a part of me I'd fought to forget. Now, this fucking letter had torn open old wounds, revealing the scars I'd hidden away.

"Why now?"

I rubbed my aching temples, the conflict within me intensifying. The Bureau had presented me with a choice—my right to privacy or the possibility of reconnecting with my long-lost son. It was a choice that shouldn't be made lightly.

Part of me wanted to protect the life I had built, to shield myself from the past I'd so desperately tried to escape. But another part of me, a part that was overshadowed by fear and uncertainty, longed to know what had become of the child I'd brought into this world.

Tears welled in my eyes and spilled onto the letter, smudging the words. It was a decision that would change the course of my life, and it felt impossible to make. I didn't even know where to begin.

The memory of Morgan's words echoed in my mind—about taking risks and being true to myself. But how could I be true to myself when I didn't even know who that self was anymore?

The room, now dimly lit by the soft glow of the lamp, felt like a sanctuary of secrets and choices. I longed for Morgan's comforting presence, but I knew I couldn't burden her with this decision just yet. It was a battle I had to face alone.

With a heavy heart, I placed the letter back in its envelope and set it on the coffee table.

"Fucking Billy Turner," I muttered, rubbing my temples. After he'd raped me, I told my parents. Of course, they blamed it on me, said I had seduced him. At the time, I blamed that horrible church they'd dragged me to. But when I discovered I was pregnant, they'd shipped me off to the Holy Spirit Sanctuary For Christian Girls.

It was a dark place, a prison of sorts located next to a swamp. It was one of many sanctuaries scattered across the country, all operated by the Pentecostal church. But this one had an especially sinister feel to it.

The rooms were sparsely decorated with crosses and Bible verses, and the staff were stern and unforgiving. We were given strict rules to follow, and I hated it there—the oppressive atmosphere and warped sense of morality suffocating me like a fog. Our days were filled with long hours of prayer and study, our evenings spent in silent obedience beneath the watchful eyes of our counselors. For entertainment, we only had bible readings and never ending sermons.

I felt like I was living in purgatory—an eternity stuck between my past mistakes and an uncertain future. My only solace came in moments when I could sneak away from prying eyes and be alone with my thoughts. During these brief moments of peace, I'd plan for my future—a future far away from this prison where I'd be free to live my life as I pleased.

"I wish I could've had an abortion," I whispered, swiping away a tear. But I didn't even know it was an option. My folks didn't want anyone to know about the baby, so I was sent there to give birth. Luckily for me, I turned eighteen a week before I went into labor. I could've left on my birthday, but I knew I wasn't keeping the child. There was no way I could support it, and I felt so detached from the baby. I felt like a walking talking baby factory, not like a mother. The boy wasn't concieved in an act of love, so why would I want a constant reminder of such a painful memory?

Labor was hell. I was scared, and in pain. But I had a plan. Three days after giving birth, I left that hellish place. Since I was over eighteen, they couldn't stop me. I lied, and told them I was going back to Georgia. But instead, I used up most of my savings and bought a bus ticket to Calilfornia. I've never spoken to my parents since, and if I ever had to see thm again, God help them.

"Honestly, I think I'd kill them." I pushed myself up from the couch, went to the bar, and came back with a tumbler of scotch.

Over the last two decades I'd only thought of the boy a handful of times. I wasn't an ogre, and despite being forced to give birth to him, I never wanted the child to suffer. Hopefully he was placed in a good home with loving parents.

I was torn between allowing my biological son to contact me and maintaining the privacy and distance I'd fought so hard for.

On one hand, there was the prospect of closure, not only for my son but also for me. Allowing contact might help me heal old wounds and answer questions that had lingered for years. There was also the chance for a reconnection, a chance to build a bridge to a part of my past I had long neglected. Perhaps there was a chance to form a bond with the child, no, he's a man now, that I'd brought into the world. I could find out if he had a good life, if he was raised in a loving family, and if he had opportunities that I couldn't have given him.

On the other hand, allowing contact would bring back the painful memories of those days in Mississippi. The decisions I had to make, and the emotional turmoil that had haunted me for so long. It would disrupt the life I'd carefully built over the years and open old wounds, exposing me to emotions and complications I wasn't prepared for.

"What would Morgan think of me if she knew I didn't want to see my own child?"

Chapter Fourteen
Morgan

The cool morning air caressed my skin as I stepped out of the hotel lobby into the Uber waiting outside.

"Good morning." I mumbled to an elderly driver. The old man grunted, then pulled away from the curb.

The sun was barely peeking up over the horizon, and I was already on my way to Paramount studios for the first day of filming. Though I was so exhausted from the early hour, I couldn't help but feel excited.

"Are you an actress?" The man's eyes met mine in the rearview mirror. "Industry folks are the only ones who get up so early in this town."

"Yes," I replied. I fished my phone out of my purse and pretended to check my messages. The old man was probably harmless, but I wasn't in the mood to talk.

The streets of Los Angeles were almost empty, the cars ahead of us moving like ghosts in the night. We were the only ones who seemed to be in a rush. I watched the city wake up from the car window - streetlights turning off, shops opening, and people emerging like shadows in the dawn sky.

When we pulled up to the studio gates, the driver let me out.

"Break a leg," he said. "That's what you people say to each other before going on stage, right?"

"Um yeah, thanks." I shut the door and flashed my pass at the guard. "I'm sorry, which way is the Echoes of Elysium set? It's so early that my brain isn't working."

"Straight ahead. Make a left at the offices, and you can't miss it." The woman pointed me in the right direction, and I hurried away, not wanting to be late on the first day of shooting.

I walked onto the set, feeling a thrill of excitement. A large movie director's chair sat in the middle of it all. Eva Thorne, the director, was glancing over a clipboard with a handsome young man. When she saw me, she grinned.

"Morgan," she said. "Glad you made it."

"Good morning," I tried to sound more awake than I was. "Where's the coffee?"

Evan laughed. "You don't have to get up so damned early on Broadway, bless your heart. Don't worry, you'll get used to it." She turned to the man next to her. "This is one of our production assistants, Ian. Dollface, take Morgan to her trailer. Oh, and you two can grab some coffee from craft services on the way. Morgan, you need to be in makeup in," she glanced at her watch. "Twenty minutes."

"This way, Ms. Sterling." Ian grinned and led me away.

I hurried after Ian, my breath hitching as I desperately tried to match his pace.

"Eva Thorne's a brilliant director, but watch your back,"

he said over his shoulder. "She can be quite the firecracker if you stay out too late - like she always does."

Ian was walking so fast I could barely keep up. I knew Eva somewhat, and what he said was true. Hopefully, this guy wasn't someone who enjoyed poking hornet nests.

"She's a brilliant director," he said, his voice louder than usual, "but she can be quite temperamental if she gets too drunk or stays out too late." I nodded as we walked, barely able to keep up with him.

"Come on," Ian said, nodding towards the craft services table. He handed me a cup of coffee, then resumed his quick pace. A few moments later, we arrive at my trailer.

"Here we are," Ian said with a wry smirk. I nodded and peered at the door. "Go on," he encouraged, "and remember, you need to be in the makeup chair in a few minutes." He handed me the key to the trailer and left.

Taking a deep breath, I grasped the handle and opened the door. The space was larger than I expected - a small bedroom separate from the living area - with walls painted in soothing shades of blue and white. A vanity sat in one corner, its shelves filled with hair and makeup stuff, while comfortable couches lined another side of the room. Even though it was only five thirty in the morning, I suddenly felt much more awake as I sipped my coffee and admired my new home away from home for the next few months.

After putting my things away, I hurried to makeup. Thankfully, my co-star Billy was already there. At least I knew someone here.

"Good morning, sleepyhead." He grinned, then gestured at the chair next to him.

"Where's the makeup people?" I asked. There was no one else here. "Eva told me to hurry, so I'd be on time."

Billy yawned, stretching his arms over his head. "Apparently, they're out of some powder they need. The woman said she'd be right back."

"I wish I could just do it myself," I said, and Billy's yawn was contagious. "It's not like they're transforming me into an alien."

"This isn't Broadway, or a low-budget picture. It's for continuity. They can't have you shooting a scene in the morning with mascara on, and in the afternoon it's gone. At least, that's what they told me when I asked about it." Billy's phone dinged, and he started tapping away. Finally, an odd-looking woman ran in and greeted me.

"Good morning! I'm Virginia," a red-haired woman said as she bustled into the trailer. She wore a vibrant floral dress that clung to her curvy frame, and her cheeks were flushed from rushing.

Virginia draped a cape over my shoulders and peered at me in the mirror. "Well now, let's get started on your makeup, shall we?" She began applying foundation with a brush, talking away as she worked.

"You know they're using all these special effects these days! It's unbelievable. Remember when shows used to be done with plain old makeup? Those were the days." She patted concealer under my eyes, then whipped out some bronzer.

The entire process took half-an hour, all to make me look natural, whatever that meant. Virginia never stopped talking, but thankfully, she didn't seem to need any responses from me.

"You're all set." She motioned for me to get out of the

chair, then she turned to Billy. "Sorry I had to keep you waiting, but Eva wants to take some stills of Morgan first thing."

"You ready for our first day, Morgan?" Billy asked.

I sipped my now cold coffee and mustered up a smile. "As ready as I'll ever be."

* * *

"Cut!" Eva shook her head. "Where the hell did you get the green screen? There's a rip in the lower left corner. Take care of it," she snapped at an assistant. "Billy, Morgan, you two can take a break. Be back on set in thirty minutes."

I hurried to my trailer. We'd been shooting for nine hours, and I prayed this interruption didn't keep us on set any longer than necessary.

When I got inside, I flopped onto the couch, exhaustion washing over me. I reached for my phone on the vanity, and as soon as I unlocked it, my heart sank. No messages from Samantha; not even a "how was your day?" text.

I sighed, trying to push away my disappointment. Then I opened up Twitter and started scrolling mindlessly through my feed, but I couldn't stop thinking about her. When I woke up alone this morning, I missed her. Yes, I knew why she didn't want to wake up at the crack of dawn, but the bed felt cold without her.

"Fuck this," I put my phone down. Obsessing over Samantha wouldn't do me any good. Instead of sitting here all by myself, I decided to grab a sandwich.

As I walked toward craft services, something strange caught my eye.

"Is that the woman I met in the elevator?" I mumbled, then

hid behind a rack of costumes.

It was Jody Agnew, walking out of Billy's trailer, sticking an envelope in her jacket pocket. What was she doing there?

My stomach dropped. Samantha and I were sure she dealt drugs. Jesus. Billy had always seemed like such a family man. But why else would he give her an envelope? I guarantee it was stuffed with cash.

After she was out of sight, I shook my head and continued walking towards the craft services table, wondering if I should confront him about it or just keep my mouth shut. It's possible he wasn't using drugs - there could have been something else in the envelope. However, did he know about that woman's shady reputation? And how the hell did she even get on our set?

I grabbed a sandwich from the craft services table and leaned against the wall as I ate, trying to decide what to do next. Ultimately, it was none of my business. And I didn't want to start a three-month film shoot on a bad foot with my co-star. The whole thing was bizarre, because when we worked together in New York, I'd never suspected he did drugs.

"Miss Sterling, you're needed on set." The assistant Ian waved at me from a few yards away.

"Be right there," I smiled, then took a last bite of the sandwich and went back to work.

* * *

"That's a wrap," Eva clapped her hands. "I'll see all of you bright and early tomorrow morning."

"I don't know what it is, but I feel like I could keep going for hours." Billy grinned. Duh. If I were on coke, I could act all night, too.

"See you at the crack of dawn," I muttered, and hurried off the set.

I finally made it to my trailer, exhausted from the day's filming. It had been a long and tiring shoot, but there was no denying that it was exhilarating. This was so much more intense than the low-budget films and tv shows I'd starred in overseas.

I quickly grabbed my phone and unlocked it with quivering fingers, hoping to see a text from Samantha. But there was nothing from her.

"Damn."

All I wanted was to hear from Samantha - to see her face, and feel her touch. I sat at the vanity and texted her. Then I dipped a sponge in a jar of cold cream and began cleaning the makeup off my face. On screen, my face appeared natural and pretty. In real life, it looked like I had a mask on.

My phone dinged, and I dropped the sponge in my hurry to see if it was Samantha.

> Sorry, but I can't see you tonight. Something's come up. I need to see you tomorrow to close on the penthouse. Text me when you're off work.

I sighed as I read the text from Samantha. Part of me was hurt that she didn't want to be with me tonight, but I knew it wasn't personal. We both had hectic schedules, and our relationship was still very new.

I slumped down onto the bed in my trailer, too tired to even change out of my costume. My eyes felt heavy, my head throbbed, and all I wanted was to sleep. Still, a part of me wished Samantha was here with me right now.

"The bed at the hotel is much more comfortable than this." I swung my legs to the floor, and a question loomed in my mind. What could possibly have "come up" for Samantha?

Chapter Fifteen
Samantha

My tired eyes drooped as I stared at the computer screen, anxiety churning in my gut. The office was eerily quiet, aside from the ticking of the clock on the wall.

I'd been trying to focus on the paperwork for the closing on Morgan's new penthouse, but I couldn't concentrate. My heart felt like someone had pulled it in two directions. On one side, I wanted to pursue a relationship with Morgan. I was falling for her, and I could easily imagine us spending our lives together. On the other side, I was scared of what she would think of me when I told her about my child.

I was so wrapped up in my thoughts that I didn't hear the knock on the door until it came a second time.

"Gray," I flinched. "You startled me."

"Looks like somebody needs more coffee." He strolled in and set a steaming cup of coffee on my desk. "You know, for someone who just sold a five-million dollar penthouse, you don't seem very excited about it."

He's right. I should be thrilled, but I had a major decision to make. The Mississippi Family Connection Bureau had sent me two letters in the last three months, and the news of my child wanting to contact me had severely thrown me off my game. Hell, I could have sold a hundred million dollar estate in Malibu and I still wouldn't get excited about it.

"Earth to Samantha," Gray waved at me. "What's eating you? You've not been yourself in months."

My heart raced as I tried to find the right words to explain my situation. How do I even begin to tell Gray that I have a child? A child I only met once after giving birth. When the nurse put the baby in my arms, I cried, but it wasn't because I was sad about giving him away. They were tears of relief because it was over, and I could get on with my life.

"Gray," I finally said. "I need to talk to you about something very important." He eyed me curiously, and then motioned for me to continue. There was no turning back now.

"This is a personal matter that I don't feel comfortable sharing with you at the office," I put my face in my hands for a moment and groaned. When I glanced at him again, a look of concern was stamped on his face. "Would you mind having a drink with me after work?"

* * *

"When did you get into bears?" I asked Gray, who shrugged. We'd just arrived at a bar called Faultline, and it was packed with gay leather daddies.

"I figured we wouldn't run into anyone we know." Gray took off his glasses and stuffed them in his pocket. "What's wrong with being into older guys?"

"Nothing." I plastered a smile on my face. "Let's find a table, someplace quiet if possible."

"Oh shit," Gray mumbled, pointing across the room. "What's she doing here?"

I followed his gaze and saw our coworker, Kim Dallin, standing with a tall, bald man. Her red hair was styled in a bob cut that made her look like even more of a vixen. She waved at us, then walked over with her friend in tow.

"Samantha!" Kim beamed as she neared us. She gave me a quick hug and paused to look Gray up and down. "Do you have contact lenses? I know you can't see shit without your glasses." Kim turned to her friend. "Bart, these are my coworkers, Samantha and Gray."

"Nice to meet you," the older man winked at Gray, who blushed. "My date just walked in, Kim. I'll talk to you later."

Gray cleared his throat and gestured towards the bar. "Can I get anyone a drink?"

Kim smiled gratefully. "That would be great! I'll have white wine, please."

"The same, please." I said.

We watched Gray disappear into the crowd before turning back to each other with raised eyebrows.

"Don't tell me you're suddenly into leather daddies?" I asked, and Kim laughed.

"No, silly. It's just easier to hang out with guys sometimes. I'm not always in the mood to be hit on at the girl bars, so I hang out with the gay guys occasionally." Kim pointed at an empty table in a corner. "Let's grab that before someone else takes it."

We rushed over and took a seat, then Gray joined us. I could feel the tension mounting between us as I tried to figure out what to say next. Despite our good relationship, I was cautious about revealing personal details in front of Kim.

"So, what's been going on lately?" Kim asked, her eyes darting between me and Gray.

Gray glanced at me before answering. "Well, not much really."

"I saw that you sold that penthouse, Samantha." Kim sipped her wine. "I showed it at least a dozen times and nobody wanted it. Good job."

Damn it. I came here to confide in Gray, not Kim. But considering Gray was the office gossip, she and everyone else I worked with would hear about it eventually.

"I consider you both to be friends," I nodded at the two of them. "What I'm about to tell you must be in the strictest confidence."

"You can trust me," Gray replied.

"Loose lips sink... shit, I forgot the rest." Kim giggled. "I promise not to breathe a word."

My mind raced as I tried to figure out the right words to tell Kim and Gray. How much should I reveal about my past? Could I trust them to keep it to themselves? It felt like there was a weight on my chest as the anxiety built up. Finally, I took a deep breath and began.

"A few months ago, I received a letter from the state of Mississippi." I picked up my glass of wine, then put it down. "I have a son I gave up for adoption when I was eighteen. He..."

"You what?" Gray's mouth dropped open.

"Whoah, that's heavy." Kim's eyes widened.

"When I got the first letter, I threw it away. For some reason, I thought if I never replied to it, nothing would happen. You know, the guy would forget about it." This was tougher than I thought. "Anyway, I got another letter a few days ago, and this time it came as certified mail. I signed for it, so now my biological child knows that I know about him." My phone pinged, so I dug it out of my purse. It was a message from Morgan. Damn, I wish I could spend time with her, but I needed to figure this problem out.

"Sorry, I need to reply to this." I tapped out a quick message, telling her I'd catch up with her tomorrow.

"So, what are you going to do?" Kim asked, and I noticed her eyes watering up. "I was adopted, and I can't imagine what your son is going through."

Shit. How could I explain my feelings about it to Kim? Could she possibly understand why I didn't want to meet him?

I grabbed my purse and stood. "Maybe I should go." I started walking away, but Kim grabbed my arm.

"Please don't run away from this," Kim pleaded. "What will you do now?"

I sighed and went back to the table, feeling my legs shaking under me. I sat down and looked at both of them, my eyes pleading for help.

"I don't know what I'm going to do," I admitted, my voice barely above a whisper. Gray put his arm around my shoulder and gave me a reassuring hug. "Samantha, you don't need to be scared of meeting him," he said softly. "You're a strong woman who has been through a lot in life. He won't hate you."

Kim nodded in agreement. "People usually find strength in difficult situations like these," she said with a kind smile on her face. Then she reached out and held my hand in hers as she continued speaking. "He's probably been through a lot in his own life, too. Chances are, he's just as scared as you are about this meeting."

Oh. My. God. They think I want to meet him.

"Kim, Gray, I don't want to meet him." A tear slid down my cheek. When I looked at Kim again, she was crying too. "I'm not a monster, I swear. But I've moved on with my life. Honestly, until I got the first letter, I'd barely thought about the child I gave up."

"How could you be so selfish?" Kim blotted her cheeks with a cocktail napkin. "Do you have any idea how lonely that boy is? I love my adopted parents, but I've spent my whole life wondering what was so fucked up about me that my mother would give me up."

"Jesus," I breathed. "Look, Kim, I..."

"There are other reasons to connect with him, too." Kim closed her eyes for a moment. "Like, he might need information about your medical history, or maybe he wasn't adopted and spent his life bouncing from one foster home to another. You might be the only family he has."

I didn't come here for this. Damn it, I wanted support, not a lecture. But Kim had a point. Maybe she'd see my point of view if I told them more about why I gave him up.

"Kim, listen to me." I reached across the table and took her hand. "When I was seventeen, I was raped."

Gray and Kim's eyes were like saucers.

"That child is a living reminder of the hell I went through. Do you really believe I want him to know that he wasn't conceived in a loving way?" I swiped away a few more tears. "That's not fair to him or me."

"I'm so sorry, Samantha," Kim squeezed my hand. "That sounds horrible. But..."

"Kim, please." Gray silenced her. "Let Samantha deal with this in the manner she sees fit."

Without a word, Kim ran off.

"Kim, please, stop..."

"Samantha, she left her purse." Gray took my hand. "Give her some time. She'll be back. If I'd known she would react this way, we could've made an excuse and gone somewhere else. But," Gray shuddered, "how were we to know? This is some seriously heavy shit."

"How do you think I feel?" Damn it. Guilt tore through me. "I've spent years getting over what happened, and now I must go through it all over again. Even if I contacted him, what if he meets me and is appalled? Do I really want to be rejected by a child I don't even know?"

"Whatever decision you make, I'm your friend and I'll stand by you, Samantha." Gray sighed.

"And how am I supposed to tell Morgan?" A tiny sob escaped me.

"Who's Morgan?" Gray reached into his pocket and put his glasses back on. He scanned the room, then pointed at a row of pinball machines. Kim was playing with one of them, and her back was turned to us. "She's over there."

"Morgan is the woman I sold the penthouse to." I sighed. "She's also my first love. We reunited recently, and I don't know how to tell her about this. I mean, look at Kim's reaction. Will Morgan think I'm a monster for not wanting to meet my child?"

Chapter Sixteen
Morgan

"Virginia, yesterday afternoon, I noticed a false eyelash coming loose. Can you use a little extra adhesive today?"

"No problem, Morgan." She smiled and started painting foundation on me.

"Want some coffee?" Billy sat next to me and handed me a cup. "I'm never getting used to being up before the roosters."

My phone pinged, and I wondered who on earth it could be so early in the morning. As soon as Virginia finished with the foundation, I pulled my phone out of my pocket and checked to see who it was.

> The paperwork is ready for you to sign. Is it possible for you to be at my office by six? If so, the seller and a rep from your bank can be here to complete the closing.

Damn, Samantha was up early.

I'll check with the director. Most likely it'll be
fine. I'll let you know within the hour.

"Looks like I'm buying my first home today," I sipped my coffee. "Well, it's actually a penthouse. Never in my wildest dreams did I ever imagine uttering those words."

"Who's your realtor?" Billy asked. "My wife and kids are driving the hotel staff insane. I thought we'd move back to New York after we're done shooting the picture, but Hollywood is rubbing off on me."

"You mean Hollyweird." Virginia chuckled. "Look up to the ceiling, Morgan."

I did as she asked and she patted concealer under my eyes.

"My realtor's name is Samantha Bishop. She works for Iconic California Estates." I felt my eyes water from staring up at the florescent lights on the ceiling. "I'm seeing her tonight. Do you want me to get a business card for you?" Hopefully, Samantha would appreciate the business.

"That would be great." Billy said.

"Good morning!" Eva bounced into the makeup trailer like she'd just drunk a pot of coffee in less than an hour. "Virginia, pay attention to her eyelashes. I noticed one of them coming loose yesterday."

"Yes, ma'am." Virginia replied. "You can look down now."

"Eva," I smiled at the director. "Is it possible I can leave by five? I need to close on my new home, and the realtor can have everyone at her office by six."

Eva frowned. "Normally, I'd say no. It's hard to predict how shooting will go. But you're in luck. We're shooting a scene with Billy this afternoon that you're not in. So if nothing comes up between now and then, it should be alright."

"Thanks!"

* * *

"Miss Sterling, congratulations. I hope you love your new penthouse." The office manager said when I told him who I was. I was still wearing makeup from today's shooting, and I thought I resembled a hooker. "Have a seat, and I'll let Samantha know you're here."

The plaque on his desk said his name was Gray. For some reason, I'd swear he was eyeing me a bit more than was necessary. Maybe he knew about me and Samantha? I sat down, and he pressed a button on his desk.

"Morgan Sterling is here Samantha. Do you want me to send her to your office?"

A moment later, she replied, "I'll come get her."

"Miss Sterling, do you want something to drink? We have anything you could want. Water, wine, even a little champagne if you're in the mood to celebrate." Gray grinned, then got to his feet.

"Water will be fine, though I might have a glass of champagne once I'm done with the closing."

Gray hurried from his desk to get me a bottle of water, and I thanked him as he handed it to me.

"I'm sure Samantha will be here shortly." He said with a smile.

The thought of finally closing on my penthouse was exciting, but even more exciting was that I would be seeing Samantha. I missed her smell and her warm embrace last night.

Just then, the door to the office opened and Samantha walked in with a smile on her face. She was wearing a tailored navy suit and had her hair pulled back into a low bun. Her beauty always took my breath away.

"Morgan!" she said happily as she reached for me, pulling me close for a hug before she let go and held me out at arm's length. "Are you ready to own your first penthouse?"

"As ready as I'll ever be," I grinned, then Gray entered the lobby and handed me a bottle of water.

"You're in expert hands, Miss Sterling," Gray winked, and in that moment I knew he knew about me and Samantha. "Is there anything else?"

"No, Gray, I'll take it from here. The bank rep and the seller are waiting for us in my office." Samantha placed a hand on the small of my back. "Come with me, Morgan."

Samantha guided me down a long corridor, her hand still resting on the small of my back. We hadn't spoken since yesterday, but that didn't make the electricity in the air any less palpable. I could feel it radiating off of her like heat from a fire.

Halfway to her office, she pulled me into a small closet. Samantha leaned in and pressed her lips to mine. Then she wrapped her arms around my waist, pulling me closer as our kiss deepened.

I felt fireworks going off inside me as I realized just how much I had missed her. Everything else melted away in that moment until all that remained was us- lost in each other's embrace in the darkness of that small closet.

Finally, Samantha pulled away with a smile on her face and took my hand, leading us out into the light once more. "God, I needed that," she said with a playful glance in my direction.

We continued down the hallway towards her office, our fingers intertwined as if we'd always been together. Jesus, it was as if time stood still, and we'd been a couple since we were teenagers.

I followed Samantha into her office, my heart pounding with anticipation. Sitting at the desk was a man in a pinstriped suit and glasses that I assumed was the bank representative. He smiled warmly as he stood to shake my hand.

"You must be Morgan!" He said cheerfully. "My name is Howard Gordon, from the Bank Of Los Angeles."

There was a woman standing beside him, dressed in a vibrant purple business suit. She was tall and slender with long dark hair and piercing blue eyes. She smiled as she held out her hand for me to shake.

"Keren Woodward," she introduced herself, with a slight British accent. "I'm the seller of your new penthouse."

We all took our seats around Samantha's desk, and Howard explained the paperwork that we had to sign in order for the sale to go through. He went through each document carefully, making sure I understood every clause before signing off on it all.

"Congratulations," Keren grinned. "Here you go," she said warmly as she handed me the keys. "Enjoy your new home."

Samantha politely showed Howard and Keren out of her office, leaving me alone with my thoughts. I couldn't help but let my mind wander. How was I going to decorate the penthouse? Would I use warm tones to make it feel cozy or go for more neutral colors with pops of accent colors throughout? I'll ask Samantha who her decorator is, because her apartment looks amazing.

Just then, Samantha returned with a bottle of champagne in one hand and two flutes in the other. She smiled mischievously as she placed them on her desk and said, "A toast. To your new home!" She popped open the bottle, and champagne spilled over her hands. "Oops," she muttered, and to my surprise, she licked her fingers clean. Perhaps she wanted to take me back to that closet? If she did, I wouldn't mind one bit.

I grabbed a flute and clinked it against hers. We took our seats once more and drank a few sips before Samantha spoke again.

"So," she said. "Tell me about your plans for the penthouse."

"Well," I began hesitantly, "I want to keep everything really classic but still modern—think marble countertops, hardwood floors, stainless steel appliances..." As I continued talking about my plans for the space, Samantha simply looked on with an amused grin on her face.

"This is my favorite part of my job, watching new home owners mentally decorate their new digs." She sipped her champagne and winked at me.

"Who decorated your apartment?" I asked. "It's really stunning."

Samantha beamed. "I did, with a little help from Gray. That boy has a wonderful eye. Maybe he'll..." Suddenly, Gray was standing in the doorway. "Speak of the devil. Morgan was asking who decorated my apartment, and I mentioned what a wonderful eye you have."

A blush warmed up Gray's pale skin. "Thanks, Samantha. Maybe I'll be able to help you, Miss Sterling."

"Morgan, please." I smiled. "Would you like a little champagne?"

"No, thanks. I have a date." Gray crossed his arms over his chest. "I just wanted Samantha to know that I'm leaving, and that everyone else is gone, too. Would you mind setting the alarm when you leave?"

"No problem, Gray." Samantha opened her arms and Gray stepped into them for a hug. I'd swear she whispered something in his ear. He blushed once more and jogged out of the room. As soon as his footsteps faded away, Samantha took my glass of champagne from me and set it on the coffee table behind her.

"We're finally alone," she purred, then she took me in her arms and kissed me. I was so taken aback by the suddenness of the kiss that all I could do was stand there, my lips still pressed against Samantha's. When I eventually found my footing and pulled away from her, I caught a glimpse of her face, which showed a soft kind of vulnerability. She smiled lightly before speaking.

"Come sit with me?"

She gestured to the sumptuous sofa behind us, and I followed her over.

The moment felt intimate as we sat side by side in silence - only broken by our gentle breaths. Low lighting illuminated us just enough that I could make out every feature on her face; the curve of her cheekbone, the arch of her eyebrows, her full lips. When she tilted towards me ever so slightly and rested her head against my shoulder, I knew there was no going back.

Our eyes locked, and without hesitation or thought, I leaned in close to kiss her again. Suddenly, there was a loud crash, like the sound of glass shattering. We froze in place for a moment, then Samantha whispered, "What the hell was that?"

Chapter Seventeen
Samantha

I grabbed Morgan's hand and pulled her up from the sofa. She looked at me with wide eyes, and I could feel the fear radiating from her.

Without a single word, I grabbed her hand and pulled her into the bathroom adjacent to my office. My heart was pounding so loudly in my chest I was sure that Morgan could hear it.

"I thought Gray said no one was here but us?" Morgan whispered.

"He did," I replied, then the sound of more glass breaking filled my ears. "I think someone broke in. Maybe they knew the alarm wasn't on yet. Shit, what the hell are they looking for? It's not like we keep cash on the premises."

We were both frozen in place, barely daring to breathe. I clung tightly to Morgan, who was trembling against me. I could feel her fear radiating off her, and it only heightened my terror.

I peered out through the crack of the bathroom door, trying to get a better view of what was going on. It sounded like someone was rummaging through my office, but it was too dark to see anything clearly. I held my breath as their footsteps came closer and closer until they eventually stopped right outside our hiding spot.

"Where the hell is it?" A woman's voice muttered. I recognized the voice from somewhere. I looked into Morgan's eyes and they widened. Did she recognize the voice too?

Suddenly, a loud crash sounded from just outside our door and we both jumped back in shock. The intruder had discovered something and was now making her way back out of the office with whatever it was they had found.

"I can't find it," the woman muttered.

The sound of feet running away from our hiding place made me breathe a little easier. After a few moments of silence, I squeezed Morgan's hand.

"I think she's gone," I whispered. "Stay here. I'm going to check things out."

"There's no fucking way I'm letting you go out there by yourself, Samantha." Morgan's voice had a brittle edge to it.

"Fine, just be quiet."

I opened the bathroom door and peered out cautiously. My office was a mess. Drawers were pulled out, papers scattered everywhere, and the bottle of champagne was gone. It was obvious someone had ransacked the place looking for something.

But what?

I felt Morgan's grip on my arm tighten as I stepped further into the room. She clearly wasn't keen on staying in our hiding spot any longer, and I didn't blame her. Morgan was terrified, and it only made me more determined to get to the bottom of this situation.

I squeezed her hand reassuringly. She'd obviously been just as scared as me, but she still came along, anyway; bravely following me into danger without question or hesitation.

That made me love her even more than before, if that was possible.

Oh my God. Did I just admit I was falling for her?

"Let's go," I whispered, tugging her gently towards the hallway where we could make our way back down the hallway. As we crept along, I kept my eyes peeled for any sign of movement or anything else out of the ordinary.

Morgan's breath hitched, and her grip on my hand tightened. She pointed down the hallway, and suddenly a shadow appeared on the wall.

I quickly pulled Morgan into the same closet we had kissed in earlier. We huddled together, hiding behind a stack of boxes. The door clicked shut, and we both held our breaths as footsteps echoed closer. I could feel Morgan trembling next to me, her body tense with fear.

My heart hammered against my chest as I tried to make out who it was and what they wanted.

Just when I thought it couldn't get any worse, the doorknob twisted, and the door opened slowly. My heart stopped for a moment and I felt Morgan stiffen in fear.

The outline of a woman appeared in the doorway, backlit by the hallway lights outside. Suddenly, I knew who she was and my stomach dropped.

Jody Agnew.

"Where the hell is it?" She muttered as she stepped into the room, scanning around for something.

I glanced at Morgan; her eyes were wide with terror. The sound of a phone vibrating startled the intruder.

"Damn it, let me fucking get the job done, asshole."

The sound of Jody leaving the closet prompted Morgan to stand up. I grabbed her hand and pulled her back down.

"Dude, I can't find it. There's no way I can keep searching. This ain't a 7-11, and I'm positive that bitch Charlotte has a state-of-the-art security system." Jody's voice grew distant. "I'm out of here!" She yelled, and I heard feet running.

We stayed in the closet, frozen in fear for a few more minutes. I could feel Morgan shaking next to me and knew I had to take action. Taking a deep breath, I opened the door and stepped out.

It was chaos; broken glass was everywhere. We moved quickly, making our way down the hallway towards my office. Once there, I grabbed my phone and dialed Charlotte's number.

My heart raced as I waited for her to pick up.

"Samantha? What's going on?" Her voice sounded panicked and confused.

"Someone broke into the office," I blurted. "I think it was Jody Agnew."

There was a long pause on the other end of the line before Charlotte spoke again.

"Are you okay?" She asked urgently.

I glanced at Morgan, who seemed to have regained her composure somewhat, but still looked shaken. "Yes," I replied, tears welling up in my eyes as relief flooded through me that we were both safe. "I'm not alone. Morgan Sterling is with me, and she can collaborate what I've told you."

"I'm hanging up now and calling the cops," Charlotte muttered. In the background, I heard Julianna ask if everything was okay. "No, someone robbed the office," Charlotte replied, then she addressed me again. "I'll be there as fast as I can, Samantha. For the love of God, stay safe."

Chapter Eighteen
Morgan

"This is a disaster," Samantha groaned. I pulled her into my arms and hugged her. "What the hell was she looking for?"

"Did I tell you about that woman at my hotel?" I asked. "The one who got on the elevator with me?"

Samantha nodded. "Yeah, Jody Agnew. It's the same woman who just trashed the office."

I stood there in shock, taking in the devastation. Everything was a mess; papers were scattered all over the floor, furniture was overturned, and the windows were smashed. Jody had done a number on the office. It was like she had gone out of her way to make sure nothing was left untouched.

"What do you think she was searching for?" I whispered, backing away from Samantha.

"Your guess is as good as mine." Samantha slowly turned around, surveying the damage. "That bitch smashed my laptop."

I stood there in shock, my mind racing with a million questions and emotions. How could someone do this? I wanted to cry, but no tears would come. My heart ached for Samantha; she looked so defeated. All I wanted to do was take her in my arms and protect her.

But what if I couldn't protect her? What if something even worse happened?

The thought terrified me. It hit me like a ton of bricks - we weren't immortal. Life was fragile and unpredictable, and anything could happen at any time.

I wasn't sure what the future held, but I knew I wanted Samantha in it. Without her, it would be incomplete. But we'd only recently reunited. Would I scare her away if I told her how much I cared for her?

"Did you hear that?" Samantha asked, then she carefully walked through shards of broken glass to the window. "Police sirens. They're on their way. C'mon, let's go to the entrance and meet them there."

Samantha and I cautiously made our way through the destroyed office, stepping over shards of glass and furniture. The destruction was unimaginable; Jody had done everything in her power to make sure nothing was left untouched.

The sign for Iconic California Estates had been spray-painted with an image of a pig. It almost looked like some kind of sick joke. What could be the point?

We made it to the entrance and saw that they had smashed the front doors in. The air was thick with tension as we stepped carefully into the reception area. Someone had overturned the desk and thrown papers all over the floor.

"What now?" Samantha whispered, her voice barely audible over the sound of police sirens in the distance.

I reached out and grabbed her hand, squeezing it gently.

"Let's wait here for help," I said firmly. "Someone will be here soon."

We stood together in silence for a few moments, watching as a police car pulled up outside and two officers got out. I felt Samantha tense up beside me as they approached, but I kept my grip on her hand tight; she wasn't alone. We were both in this together, no matter what happened next.

"Ladies," an older man in a rumpled brown suit greeted us. "I'm Detective Jones, and this is Officer Porter. Please remain where you are while we look around."

A moment later, an elegant woman with porcelain skin and red hair walked in.

"Oh my God," she mumbled. "Thank God they didn't hurt you, Samantha." She hugged her, then turned to me. "I'm so sorry you were here when this happened. You are Morgan Sterling?"

"Yes." I crossed my arms over my chest. "It was terrifying."

"My name is Charlotte Adams." A tear slid down her cheek. "This is my life's work, and somebody tried to destroy it."

"I know who did it." Samantha frowned.

"Do you really?" The detective sauntered back into the reception area. "Please, tell me everything you know."

"Detective Jones, it's good to see you again." Charlotte attempted a smile. She turned to me. "Detective Jones helped put away Bart Holstein. You might recognize the name."

"Oh wow, you're that Charlotte Adams?" I eyed her curiously. "It was all over the news what you did to put him behind bars."

The other police officer returned and whispered in the detective's ear.

"Ladies, apparently the perpetrator left what appears to be an employee break room untouched. Why don't we go there and I can ask you all a few questions." The detective nodded at the policeman. "Officer Porter, stay here and wait for the forensics team."

* * *

Samantha glared at Detective Jones with tear-filled eyes. "I know it was Jody Agnew," she said, her voice cracking. "We never saw her face, but I recognized her voice. Morgan recognized it too."

"Miss Sterling, how do you know Jody Agnew?" The middle-aged man drew his bushy eyebrows together. "Please, tell us everything you know."

"The first time I saw her, Samantha and I were at The Velvet Vixen," I said, and the detective scribbled in a notebook. "Samantha pointed her out and said she was Miss Adams' ex-girlfriend."

Charlotte paled.

"The next time was at my hotel. At least I think it was her." I shut my eyes for a moment, trying to recall all the details. "It was at the front desk at the Chateau Marmont. She claimed she had a package for Declan Montgomery and tried to get them to give her his room number. They refused, then a few minutes later when I got on the elevator, she was on it too." I must have made a face, because Samantha took my hand. "She was, well, very forward with me, if you know what I mean."

"That sounds like her," Detective Jones sighed.

"Detective," a woman wearing latex gloves stepped into

the break room. "I was able to look at footage from the security cameras before they were damaged. The perp knows what they're doing. I couldn't get a single good look at them. They wore a ski mask, gloves, and..."

"That distinctive leather jacket," the detective chimed in. "Ms. Agnew has been on our radar for a long time, but we can never make anything stick. But, without witnesses..."

"We heard her voice, I swear!"

Samantha's grip on my hand tightened.

"Miss Sterling, this is valuable information," the detective said. "It establishes a connection between you, Samantha, and the suspect. We'll need to look into her activities more closely."

Samantha chimed in, her voice more determined now. "Detective, I'm convinced Jody is trying to get back at Charlotte. She put her boss, Bart Holstein, behind bars, and, you know, Jody was involved in all kinds of illegal shit. Charlotte helped bring her to justice."

"I was the detective on that case, and I'm fully aware of who we're dealing with." Detective Jones shrugged.

Charlotte nodded, her face grave. "I was always afraid Jody might come back for revenge. I'll cooperate fully with the investigation. If there's anything I can do to help, please let me know."

The detective closed his notebook and looked at all of us. "Thank you for your cooperation. We'll do our best to solve this case and bring the perpetrator to justice. It's clear we're dealing with a skilled individual, but with your help, we might just get a lead. Please stay in touch, and if you remember anything else, don't hesitate to contact us."

* * *

"... Julianna, I'll be home in a little while. I have to contact our insurance company and figure out what to do about all this damage. Did you look at the photos I sent you?" Charlotte was pacing through the reception area, deftly avoiding the debris. "It's tragic. Alright love, I'll see you soon." She disconnected the call and turned to me and Samantha. "I'm worried for both of you. Please tell me you won't be alone tonight."

"No," Samantha turned to me. "Morgan and I will stay together."

"Where the hell is Gray?" Charlotte muttered. "He knows where everything is, but he isn't returning my..."

"Wow," Gray strolled in, and his mouth dropped open. "This is unbelievable." He slowly turned around, taking in the destruction. When he saw me, he grimaced. "I hate to tell you this, but you're on The Hollywood Gossip Zone, and a few other websites." He held out his phone.

"What?" Samantha snatched the phone out of his hand. "Oh my God." Samantha handed me the phone. "Read this."

Broadway Star Morgan Sterling Caught in Shocking Robbery at Iconic California Estates!

The red carpets of Tinseltown have been rolled up, and the spotlight has shifted to a different kind of drama in the City of Angels. Our favorite Broadway sensation, the talented Morgan Sterling, who graced the stages of New York with her incredible performances, is now making waves on the West Coast. But not for the reasons you might think!

Morgan Sterling, known for her mesmerizing presence on the Broadway stage, is currently in Los Angeles to shoot the film adaptation of "Echoes of Elysium," the play she starred in last year. However, she recently found herself at the center of a real-life Hollywood heist that could rival any blockbuster script.

The stunning starlet was at the scene of a jaw-dropping robbery at the headquarters of the prestigious real estate firm, Iconic California Estates. Sterling was not the target, but she was there during the shocking event, and our sources say it was a harrowing experience. ••

Rumors are flying, and the plot thickens as Morgan Sterling's connection to the incident raises eyebrows. Was it mere coincidence, or is there more to this story than meets the eye? 🕵️

The criminal mastermind behind the robbery remains a mystery, shrouded in a ski mask. Could this be a devious move from someone within Sterling's inner circle? We can't help but speculate!

Our sources reveal that Sterling had a close encounter with the suspect in the elevator at the luxurious Chateau Marmont. Could this be a case of mistaken identity or something far more sinister? 😨

The star-studded cast of "Echoes of Elysium" is surely in for a whirlwind of Hollywood drama on and off the set. Stay tuned as we follow this story closely, bringing you all the juicy details, as the dazzling Morgan Sterling navigates the glitz and glamor of the film industry alongside the shadowy secrets of the City of Angels.

It's a Hollywood mystery fit for the silver screen, and we can't wait to see how it all unfolds!

"How did they find out about this so fast?" I handed Gray his phone back. "I mean, I haven't even gone back to the hotel yet."

"This is Hollywood," Gray shrugged. "From what I see, their source knows you met the suspect in an elevator at your hotel. It's probably someone on the police force who fed the story to the gossip sites."

"Jesus, I should move back to New York." I wrapped my arms around myself. "This is insane."

Samantha put her arm around my waist. "Honey, I'm staying with you tonight."

A tiny sob escaped me. "But Jody knows where I'm staying. What if she tries to hurt us?"

Chapter Nineteen
Samantha

"It's going to be okay," I breathed, and took Morgan's hand. "You will stay at my place tonight. I don't think Jody knows where I live."

"Well, I don't know about the rest of you, but I could use a stiff drink." Gray said. "Charlotte, why don't you get Julianna to meet us somewhere for a cocktail?"

Charlotte looked up at him sharply and then glanced at me. When she saw my nod, she excused herself and pulled out her phone.

"Tell her to meet us at The Frolic Room in an hour." Gray pulled out his phone. "Actually, we should get everyone who works here to join us. Otherwise, some of them might show up here tomorrow morning and freak out. It's not every day that your office becomes a crime scene." He followed Charlotte out of the room, leaving me and Morgan alone.

"I'm so sorry this happened to us, baby." I tightened my grip on Morgan's hand. "But trust me, I'm not letting anything happen to you."

"Trust?" Morgan pulled me in for a hug, then whispered in my ear. "I think you're the only person in the world I trust right now."

* * *

The bright neon lights of The Frolic Room illuminated the night as we stepped from the backseat of Gray's car. I steadied Morgan as she wobbled slightly on her feet, her eyes still red from crying.

"Go on inside," Gray said as he glanced around for a parking spot. "I'll be there in a minute."

I nodded, and looped my arm through Morgan's, guiding her towards the entrance of the bar. As we walked in, I looked around at the eclectic decor and wondered if this was a good idea. There were some pretty shady characters here, and I wasn't sure if I wanted to bring Morgan anywhere near them.

But then again, it didn't look like we had much choice right now - and we both needed a stiff drink after all that had just happened back at the office. So I guided us over to an empty table in the corner and took a seat next to her.

She grabbed my hand under the table and squeezed it. I squeezed back reassuringly and glanced around for Charlotte or Julianna - maybe they were already here waiting for us? Just then Gray walked in with Julianna in tow - followed by Charlotte, who looked wildly out of place in this dive bar.

Gray went to the bar with Charlotte, and a few moments later, they came to our table.

"Here you are," Charlotte said warmly as she handed us our drinks - whiskey sours - then sat down across from us with her own martini glass filled with icy vodka.

Gray sat next to Julianna and Charlotte, then pulled out his phone. "Oh my God, the gossip sites are losing their minds." He handed Morgan the phone, and I leaned over and read the story with her.

Broadway Star Morgan Sterling Injured in Daring Robbery at Iconic California Estates!

Glamour Turns to Grit as Sterling Fights Off Intruders

Hollywood, CA—*Drama unfolded at the prestigious Iconic California Estates as beloved Broadway sensation Morgan Sterling, famous for her enchanting performances, found herself in a real-life thriller. The star was injured during a shocking attempted robbery at her luxurious estate last night.*

"What luxurious estate?" Morgan muttered.

Sources close to the incident reveal that Sterling put up a fierce fight as the intruders tried to gain access to her dazzling jewelry collection. Reports suggest that her quick thinking and bravery may have thwarted the thieves' sinister plans.

"Can I have your emerald and sapphire tiara, darling?" I teased, and for the first time all night, a small smile spread across Morgan's cheeks.

The Hollywood hills were lit up with sirens as the fearless starlet managed to call for help before the culprits made a clean getaway. Sterling's resilience shone through, earning her applause from both fans and the authorities.

While the extent of her injuries remains undisclosed, her fans are anxiously awaiting updates on her condition. Sterling's bold stand against the would-be robbers has only added to her reputation as a true heroine. She's currently in Hollywood shooting the film version of the hit Broadway play, Echoes of Elysium.

Stay tuned for more as the investigation unfolds, and Broadway's darling, Morgan Sterling, recovers from this shocking incident.

I glanced up to see Kim Dallin standing in the doorway of the bar. Her eyes fell on me and she frowned.

"Judgemental bitch," I muttered, and Morgan's eyebrows drew together. "It's nothing, just ignore me."

Without another glance at me, Kim walked up to the bar and ordered herself a drink.

"Well, the gang's all here," Charlotte murmured, and less than a minute later, we were making room at the table for Lucy and Kim.

"Oh my God!" Lucy cried when she sat down. "What the hell happened? It's all over the news about the break in."

Kim's eyes fell on me, and she frowned. Jesus, why the hell did I think I could trust her with my secret?

I took a deep breath and forced a smile. It was time to introduce Morgan to Lucy and Kim. I knew this could be tricky; Kim already knew about the child I gave up for adoption, and I didn't want her to say anything about it in front of Morgan.

I winked at Kim, silently asking her to keep her mouth shut about the secret I had shared with her the night before. She frowned, but thankfully she seemed to understand what I was asking for without me having to spell it out.

"Kim, Lucy, this is Morgan Sterling." I put my arm over Morgan's shoulder. "She bought the penthouse I sold, and unfortunately for her, was at the office when the break in occurred."

"Hi, Morgan," Kim held her hand out. "I'm Kim."

Morgan smiled politely and shook her hand. "Nice to meet you," she said.

"This is Lucy," I said. "She also works at ICE."

"Nice to meet you, Morgan." Lucy shook her hand, then exclaimed, "What the hell happened?"

Everyone turned to Charlotte. She took Julianna's hand and began to explain about the robbery. When she was done, Kim eyed her.

"Did the robber actually take anything?"

A curious expression settled on Charlotte's face. "Actually, I don't know. From the looks of things, they just vandalized the office. It's a total disaster, and none of you can return to work until the insurance people and the police have gone over everything with a fine-toothed comb. Tomorrow, we all work from home, so expect a few Zoom calls."

"We heard her speaking to someone on a phone," I grimaced. "She was definitely searching for something."

"And you're positive it was Jody Agnew?" Julianna asked.

"Yes," Morgan and I spoke at the same time.

"You know she'll probably get away with it," Charlotte's fists clenched. "She's like that childhood saying come to life. I'm rubber, and you're glue. Whatever you throw at me will bounce off and stick to you. Or at least I think that's how that saying goes."

"Close enough," I drawled, then I glanced over at Kim. She was scowling, and I wasn't sure if it was aimed at me, or if it was because of the break-in.

I felt a wave of guilt wash over me at the thought of Kim knowing my secret. I had entrusted her with this information, and she hadn't betrayed me or said anything to anyone else about it. But still, the knowledge weighed heavily on my mind.

If Kim didn't like me because of what I did, I didn't give a damn. Only after she walked a few thousand miles in my pumps would I even consider letting her disapproval get to me.

"Earth to Samantha." Morgan waved her hand in front of my face. "Honey, do you want another drink?"

I noticed all eyes were on us, probably because they didn't know we were dating. Were we dating? What exactly was happening between us?

"Yeah, but only one more." I smiled, then Gray stood up and went to the bar.

I knew that eventually I would have to tell her about my past, but when? It seemed too soon to bring it up now, especially when we were just getting to know each other again. But I wanted our relationship to be based on trust and genuine honesty, not secrets and hidden truths.

It seemed like an impossible task. How was I supposed to navigate this delicate situation without causing pain or discomfort for either of us? How was I supposed to reach out and bridge the gap between my past and our present?

For the time being, I decided it would be best for both of us if I kept my secret from Morgan for now. There would come a time when she needed to know the truth, but for now it could wait until the right moment presented itself and everything felt right between us.

Until then, all I could do was move forward with caution and make sure that my actions in the present never betrayed my troubled past.

* * *

I felt my muscles relax as I settled into bed, the warmth of Morgan's body next to me like a comforting blanket. We had just finished hanging out with my co-workers and I was tired and slightly drunk from the few drinks I had earlier.

My eyes were already growing heavy when Morgan's phone began ringing. She groaned as she looked at the caller ID, then sighed before picking up.

"Hi Eva," she croaked, her voice full of exhaustion. "Of course, I don't have a luxurious estate or major jewelry." Morgan giggled, and I heard her director laughing. Morgan said nothing for a few moments as she listened to Eva, then Morgan sighed. "Thank you. I'll see you at the crack of dawn next Monday morning. Bye." Morgan placed the phone on the nightstand and snuggled against me. "Well. Eva has given me a few days off to recuperate. What she didn't say was thanks for the free publicity."

"What do you mean?"

"The story is all over the gossip sites, and almost all of them mention that I'm in Hollywood shooting *Echoes of Elysium*." Morgan yawned. "I'm surprised my agent hasn't called." She sat up in bed, grabbed her phone, and punched a few buttons. "There. I don't want him to wake us up in the middle of the night."

Morgan laid down again, this time putting her head on my chest. "Thank you," she whispered. "I..."

I looked down at Morgan, her eyes soft and radiating with emotion. She seemed to be on the brink of saying something, but was hesitating like she was scared of my reaction. I could see she was struggling with something, so I gently placed my hand on her shoulder in an effort to encourage her.

"What were you going to say?" I asked softly.

Morgan took a deep breath and exhaled slowly before responding. "Thank you," she whispered, her voice barely more than a whisper. "I couldn't have survived this without you."

No matter how much she tried to brush it off, I could tell there had been something else that she had been about to say; something that made her hesitant and vulnerable all at once.

Gently lifting her chin up so that our eyes met again, I said in a comforting voice, "Morgan, you know that whatever it is— you can tell me."

"Today's been so intense," Morgan draped her arm over my waist. "Let's get some sleep."

My heart was pounding in my chest as I watched Morgan drift off to sleep. As much as I wanted to deny it, I knew what I was feeling for her was more than just simple lust; it was something more. And I had a feeling that she felt the same way about me, too.

But what if Morgan finds out about my past and the baby that I gave up for adoption? Would she understand why I don't want to contact him? Would she still feel the same way about me? My head was spinning with a million different questions and worries, but no matter how hard I tried to come up with answers, all that kept coming into focus were two simple words: "What if?"

As if sensing my inner turmoil, Morgan stirred beside me and shifted closer, wrapping her arm around my waist as she let out a soft snore. The sound of her contented breathing eventually lulled me into sleep. As darkness slowly crept in around us, the only thought lingering in my mind before finally succumbing to fatigue was: will Morgan be able to accept all of me? Including the choices I've made?

Chapter Twenty
Morgan

My eyes fluttered open to the bright morning sun flooding into the room. It's much later than usual, I can tell, and a wave of relief washed through me. I usually have to be up before the sun even thinks of rising, rushing to the studio for an early shoot. But this morning, I'm still nestled in the warmth of Samantha's arms, her steady breath rumbling through my body.

I take a moment to savor this peaceful moment, but then reality floods back in with a shudder. I vividly remember what happened yesterday - the robbery at Samantha's office, the fear on her face, and the desperation we both felt. I'm thankful that no one was hurt, but the memory still leaves a sour taste in my mouth.

My heart aches as I turned to face Samantha. I can't help but think of how close I came to telling her I loved her right before we fell asleep last night. But it wasn't the right time, and I don't want to put any extra pressure on Samantha. I just want her to know that I'm here for her.

Samantha stirred in her sleep and I felt her arms tighten around me.

"Good morning sunshine," I giggled, and Samantha's eyes fluttered open. "I haven't slept this late in a long time."

"What time is it?" Samantha yawned.

My heart sank as I picked up my phone from the nightstand. I knew what would happen when I turned off airplane mode - an onslaught of messages from people in the entertainment industry. As soon as my phone switched on, it came alive in my hands, vibrating and buzzing relentlessly with a never-ending stream of messages.

"Shit!" I exclaimed, dropping it back onto the nightstand in surprise.

Samantha stirred beside me and asked groggily, "What's going on?"

I sighed heavily. "The news about the robbery," I said grimly. "Everyone knows now."

Samantha gasped and sat bolt upright in bed, grabbing her phone to check the news for herself. Her face turned pale and her eyes widened in shock as she read the robbery stories online.

My personal inbox was now overflowing with emails and text messages from producers, directors, agents, managers - everyone who had ever worked with me wanted to know what had happened and if I was okay.

Samantha opened up the drawer to the nightstand next to her and dropped her phone inside.

"Give me your phone," she ordered, and I handed it to her. Samantha placed it in the drawer with her phone and shut it. "No phones until after we've at least had a cup of coffee."

"But what if..."

I tried to suppress a smile as Samantha's hand slid under my panties and touched my inner thigh. Her lips pressed against the back of my neck, sending chills down my spine.

"Morgan, darling," she murmured, her breath hot on my skin. "I can't even think straight yet. Just give us a little more time before we allow the world to intrude on us." Samantha rolled me over and both of us giggled.

As we stared at each other, a mischievous glint sparked in Samantha's eyes. She sat up, her blonde hair falling over her bare shoulders like a waterfall of silk. I watched as she bit her lower lip, that sensual gesture sending a jolt of electricity down my spine to the core of my desire.

"No need for getting out of bed yet," she purred seductively, her voice husky with sleep. The implicit suggestion hung in the air between us like the sweetest perfume, denying it seemed impossible.

She playfully reached under my panties, and I felt the heated flush of our desire spread across my skin like wild fire.

Her hands traced a path on my abdomen under the fabric, triggering flutters of anticipation that sent shivers down my legs. "What about breakfast?" I murmured amidst gasps as her fingers dipped lower.

She grinned as her fingers danced teasingly around my folds. "Who needs food when there's dessert?" she whispered sultrily into my ear, her tongue flicking lightly against my earlobe before nipping it gently.

A moan escaped me, emboldening her actions further. With a few assertive tugs, she rid me of the nightgown, leaving nothing but skin against skin. My body arched instinctively towards hers as she moved lower slowly, savoring every inch of my exposed flesh with her lips and teeth.

"Samantha," I gasped out breathlessly, clutching tightly onto the bedsheet beneath. Her actions spurred on by the sultry fervor in my voice, she traced a path down to the apex of my thighs with her tongue, her hands settling on my hips to steady me against her mouth's assault. The pleasure was dizzying under her expert ministrations. My hands instinctively tangled into her hair, pulling her closer and encouraging her to delve deeper.

Our moans and whimpers echoed around the room as Samantha explored my pussy, each flick of her tongue escalating us both towards ecstasy. "Don't stop," I gasped in a shaky whisper that was barely audible over the throb of my own heartbeat pounding in my ears.

She responded by adding a finger, then two to the mix; the dual pleasure making me writhe uncontrollably beneath her touch. Pressure built within me, expanding like an insistent wave until it broke with shattering intensity.

"Oh, God, yes!" I moaned.

We laid intertwined on the rumpled bedsheets, chests heaving and bodies slick with perspiration. We basked in the afterglow of our lovemaking, and for those few stolen moments, nothing else mattered - no robbery, no calls or texts; just us.

"C'mon," I said reluctantly once our breathing had normalized somewhat. "Let's go make some breakfast." Samantha nestled herself even closer against me in response and mumbled something about 'second helpings' against my collarbone, sending us both into a bout of giggly laughter.

As we recovered from our morning tryst, a rush of emotions surged through me. I was falling for her - deeply and irrevocably and, as much as I wanted to tell her so, fear of rejection kept me from voicing the words. We'd only just reunited after years apart; it would be all too easy to spoil the precious moment by saying too much.

I inched closer to her, gently tracing the outline of her jaw with my fingertips. I wanted nothing more than to spend every single second with her, to laugh together, cry together, make love. My feelings were overwhelming but beautiful at the same time, and despite the uncertainty that hung in the air, I was determined not to jinx what we had by voicing them out loud yet.

"What's going on in that beautiful head?" Samantha breathed. "Jody isn't going to hurt us, I promise."

"Jody?" I was confused for a second, probably because I just woke up and had a mind-blowing orgasm. "Oh, um, yeah. As long as we're together, that creature can't harm us."

Samantha's brow furrowed. "Is there something else on your mind?"

I'd swear Samantha could read my thoughts. It's like she knew I was thinking about us. A smile split my face.

"Why are you smiling like that?" Samantha kissed my cheek.

Because there is now an us.

"I'm starving, and I love nothing more than to cook." I threw back the covers and leapt out of bed. "I hope you have food in the fridge."

I whipped up the perfect omelette to start off our breakfast. I couldn't help but smile as I added a few herbs and spices for flavor.Samantha set the dining room table for two. She'd set out a plate of fresh fruit along with pancakes and bacon. I could get used to domestic bliss, and I prayed Samantha enjoyed it, too.

Samantha took a seat at the table and motioned for me to join her.

"Everything smells delicious. You're a much better chef than me."

As we sat down together, I felt something special in the air between us — an intangible connection that seemed to grow stronger by the second.

"Since we both have the day off, what do you want to do?" I asked. "Something we've never done before, or..."

"We need to go to my office and pray the cops let us in. The keys to your penthouse and all the paperwork are still there." Samantha sipped her coffee. "And I need to check in with Charlotte to see if I'm needed for anything. Since we closed on your place yesterday, she might want me to start working on another property."

"Ooh, I forgot about the penthouse," I giggled. "So much happened yesterday. If Charlotte doesn't need you, how would you like to go furniture shopping with me? Oh, and I'm not into contemporary furnishings. I'm a vintage girl. Let's go to the best thrift stores in town and see what we can find."

Samantha grinned. "That sounds like a great idea. We can make a day of it and find some unique pieces to give your penthouse an individual touch. I'm sure you'll be able to find something that suits your style."

"Well, for starters," I rubbed my hands together. "I want it to be inviting, but also modern and eclectic. Lots of texture too - fluffy rugs and cushions in jewel tones, plus metal accents for an edgy vibe."

Samantha nodded. "What about hanging up a gallery wall? That would look really cool."

"Oh my gosh, yes!" I practically squealed with excitement at this brilliant suggestion. "That would be perfect! And what about plants? Some flowers will add life and energy into the space." I could talk for hours about decorating. "Can we stop by my hotel first so I can pick up some clothes?"

Damn. I practically just invited myself to stay here for a few days.

"That sounds perfect." Samantha stood. "Since you cooked, I'll do the dishes."

She started clearing the table while I raced to the kitchen and poured another cup of coffee. After passing Samantha on her way to the kitchen, I sauntered through the living room, admiring the décor as I went. An antique wooden buffet against one wall caught my eye and, upon closer inspection, I noticed a crisp white envelope with a government seal lying on top of it.

Curiosity got the better of me and I picked up the envelope. It was from the Mississippi Family Connection Bureau.

"Morgan," Samantha's voice came from behind me. "I'll take that."

Chapter Twenty-One
Samantha

I couldn't believe my eyes as I stared at the envelope in Morgan's hands. My heart raced, and I prayed I didn't have a panic attack. I knew I had to take it, but the thought of what this could mean was daunting.

Morgan glanced up at me, her eyes full of concern. "I'm sorry, I didn't know..."

"No big deal." I said, trying to keep my voice even. I took the envelope from Morgan and kissed her on the cheek. "Just a little problem. I have to work on by myself."

Inside, I was crumbling. I was scared—scared that Morgan would leave me if she found out the truth, that I didn't want to meet my biological child. Reuniting with him would devastate me, rocking the foundations of the life I'd made for myself on my own.

"You know you can trust me, don't you?" Morgan's eyes lowered to the envelope in my hand. "Does it have something to do with the group home in Mississippi you told me about?"

As I stared down at the envelope in my hands, I felt a knot form in my stomach. It wasn't that I was frightened of what it contained—I already knew. But having Morgan know the truth...I just couldn't bring myself to do it.

Yet.

My thoughts drifted back to my teenage years spent in the group home in Mississippi, and how ashamed and embarrassed I'd been to tell anyone about it. The whispers behind my back, the looks of pity—it was all too much for me. Even now, all these years later, it still gave me chills to think about it.

"Are you okay, Samantha?" Morgan laid her hand on my arm.

I wanted to tell Morgan everything—but at the same time, part of me wanted her to never know the truth. How could she possibly understand what I'd gone through? But the thought of lying to her was even worse than telling her—would she ever forgive me if she found out?

"So... what is it?" Morgan asked softly, breaking into my thoughts. She eyed me closely as if trying to read my mind, and suddenly I realized how unfair this whole situation was—to both of us.

"It's... nothing," I said finally with a forced smile. "Just something private." Glancing up at Morgan's worried expression, I took her hand in mine and grinned reassuringly. "Come on," I mumbled. "Let's get dressed and go shopping."

* * *

Morgan and I stepped inside a vintage thrift store in West Hollywood called The Hipster Haven Emporium. I was immediately taken by the array of treasures. From funky furniture to vintage clothes and books, this place was a hidden gem —I could just imagine all the stories these items must have to tell.

Morgan grinned, her eyes sparkling with delight as she surveyed the thrift store's offerings. "Look at this!" she exclaimed, pointing to an old chest of drawers. "This would be perfect for my penthouse. It would be a snap to refinish it."

We made our way around the shop, picking up items here and there that we thought would fit Morgan's vision of her dream home. Morgan admired the intricate details on some of the furniture pieces, while I looked through racks of blouses and skirts with a critical eye.

"Look at this!" I pointed at an ancient rotary dial phone painted in vibrant colors. "I love it."

"You, my dear, have excellent taste. Now come with me." Morgan looped her arm through mine, and we strolled through the store together.

"What do you think of this one?" I asked her, admiring a beautiful vase. She smiled and nodded. "Oh, it would look perfect with forest green silk curtains." As we moved on, I imagined ourselves living like any other happy couple.

But then my thoughts drifted back to that envelope tucked away in my pocket—the one containing news about a past I'd rather forget forever. It seemed so wrong to keep something from Morgan...but before I could think too much about it, Morgan distracted me by pointing out a beautiful wall hanging made of bright fabric scraps stitched together with colorful yarns and ribbons.

"Isn't this gorgeous?" She asked with admiration in her

voice. "My grandmother in Bucharest used to make stuff like this."

"I love folk art." I spied a stunning painting across the room. "Morgan, I'm going to look at a painting. I'll be back in a moment."

"Most of the furniture is in the rear of the store. Come find me when you're done." She kissed my cheek, then strolled away.

The painting was like many others I'd seen over the years in southern California. It was a large, abstract canvas filled with bold strokes of warm hues—deep oranges, magentas, and golds—that evoked the feeling of a California sunset. The artist's signature was barely visible in the corner, adding an air of mystery to this secondhand gem. The frame didn't match the painting, but it added to its charm. "If Morgan doesn't like it, I'll take it."

I picked up the painting and turned to go find her, but when I saw her, I almost dropped it to the floor.

Jody Agnew was only a few feet away from her.

"Shit," I muttered, and hid behind a shelf full of old books. What the hell was she doing here? Was she stalking us?

My hands shook as I pulled my phone out of my purse. I dialed the cops, and soon a voice on the other end said, "911. What is your emergency?"

"I'm at an antique store in Burbank called The Hipster Haven Emporium," I whispered into the phone. "There's someone here that was involved in a robbery yesterday where I work, Iconic California Estates. Her name is Jody Agnew."

"Are you sure it's her?" the man's voice asked calmly.

"Yes. Absolutely," I replied, struggling to keep my voice under control.

"Okay," the officer said. "What's your location, again?" My heart raced as I gave him all the details and described what Jody was wearing: a blue t-shirt, jeans, and a scuffed black leather jacket.

"We'll be there as quickly as possible. Stay where you are until a patrol car gets there." The officer disconnected the call.

I quickly surveyed the area for an escape route in case Jody spotted me or tried to make a run for it. However, she seemed completely unaware of my presence as she followed Morgan near the back of the store.

Damn it, should I rush over to make sure she's okay, or should I hang back and wait for the cops to show up? So far, Morgan hadn't seen Jody. Suddenly, Morgan's head swiveled around, probably searching for me. Instead, she saw Jody, who was staring straight at her.

"Oh my God!" Morgan yelled, dropping an antique vase. It crashed to the floor, breaking into pieces. Jody grinned at her, then she took off running for the exit.

She apparently didn't see me, because she was running down the aisle toward my hiding place. There's no way I was letting her out of here without a fight. I took a deep breath and stood up straight.

"Stupid bitch," Jody growled, then pushed me out of the way. A store clerk stepped into the aisle, blocking Jody.

"What's going on here?" The clerk was an older black man with dreadlocks hanging to his waist. Jody didn't stop running. When she got to the man, she elbowed him in the side, and he knocked over a shelf full of old pots and pans.

My heart pounded as I watched Jody make a break for the exit. She seemed determined to get away, but two police officers stepped into the store just in time to block her path.

"Hold up there," one of them said, raising his hand. His partner stood next to him, his body a solid wall of authority. "We're taking you in for questioning."

Jody stopped and slowly turned around. Her face was pale and her eyes were wide with fear. "What? What did I do?" she stammered.

The officer closest to Jody stepped forward and said, "You have the right to remain silent. Anything you say can and will be used against you in a court of law. You have the right to an attorney. If you cannot afford one, one will be provided for you." He handcuffed her, the metallic clicks echoing through the store.

Turning towards the second officer, he looked at Morgan and me with concern. "Are you both okay?" he asked.

I nodded, my grip on Morgan's hand firm. "Yeah, we're fine. Thanks for the quick response."

The officer nodded, his gaze serious. "We'll need you both to come down to the station later to give your statements. Make sure to mention any previous incidents or threats from the suspect. It'll help with the case."

Morgan and I exchanged a glance. "We'll be there. Thank you for handling this," I said.

"Do any of you know this woman?" he asked, pointing at Jody as she was being led away by the other officer.

"I'm the one who called 911." I stepped forward and realized Morgan was now by my side. "Iconic California Estates was burglarized yesterday, and we think that woman had something to do with it. Her name is Jody Agnew, and she has a history with my boss, Charlotte Adams. I saw her sneaking up behind Morgan." I nodded at her. "I swear she's stalking us, officer. She keeps showing up wherever we go."

The officer rubbed his chin and sighed. "Do you know why she's stalking you?"

Chapter Twenty-Two
Morgan

"I'm not sure." Samantha glanced over at me, a worried look in her eyes. "I think Jody's more concerned about hurting my boss, Charlotte. We don't have a history with the woman. But ever since Charlotte helped put Jody's buddy Bart Holstein in prison, Jody keeps showing up." Samantha swiped at her eyes.

The officer scribbled in a tiny notebook with a chewed up pencil, then he tucked it away into his pocket. "My name is Officer Hellman. Ladies, I don't know what you've gotten yourselves into, but please come down to the station and provide us with an official statement. It'll create a paper trail, so if you end up needing to secure a restraining order against Jody Agnew, there'll be proof that something happened."

I took a deep breath and glanced at Samantha. Her eyes were heavy and her skin was pale. Nodding, I said, "You're right. We should do as he says. Otherwise, who knows when this psycho will show up again?"

She nodded weakly, and I pulled her closer to me.

"It's better than sitting around doing nothing."

* * *

I shifted in my seat as we pulled out of the parking lot, feeling a heavy weight pressing down on my shoulders. The cops told us to report to the police station and provide an official statement, and that's what we were doing. Although I was scared of Jody and what she might do, I was more scared of the thought of her getting away with it. We needed to provide a record so that if she shows up again; we have proof that something happened.

The car was silent as Samantha drove us towards the station. I couldn't help but think about how easily Jody popped up wherever we went—it made me feel vulnerable. I glanced over at Samantha; her normally vibrant face had turned pale and her eyes were heavy with worry. She seemed as afraid as I felt, but there was also determination in her expression. She didn't want Jody to get away with this, either.

I took a deep breath and looked out of the window, watching the cityscape pass by in a blur. My heart sank when I saw the looming silhouette of the police station ahead of us; it was almost like a reminder of just how serious this situation was becoming. We were about to give our statements under oath, and there was no turning back now. With a heavy sigh, I closed my eyes for a moment and prayed that this would all be over soon.

Samantha pulled the car into a parking spot at the police station and shut off the engine. She turned to me and said, "After we're done with this, I need to have a serious discussion with you."

I nodded, knowing that she was referring to Jody Agnew and the situation we were in. Just then, a blue Mercedes S Class pulled into the lot. It was Samantha's boss, Charlotte, accompanied by her wife Julianna. They got out of their car and strolled over to us.

"We're here to provide moral support," Charlotte said firmly, taking both my hands in hers. "You don't have to go through this alone."

I returned her smile gratefully as Samantha wrapped an arm around me in a comforting hug. Although I still felt scared of what might happen when we talked to the police, their presence made me feel a little better about it all.

"I've never been to a police station before," I mumbled. "Why is this happening now? I get my first big break in Hollywood, and now we have some crazed stalker hounding us."

"Let's go," Charlotte murmured, making her way towards the entrance of the station. Samantha and Julianna flanked my sides protectively as we walked up the steps together. Charlotte opened the door and waited for the three of us to pass before following along behind us.

We strolled down a hallway until we were in a beige, dreary lobby. I was so scared that I could barely think straight; all I wanted to do was turn around and run back out of the station.

But I knew that wasn't an option anymore. It was time to face this head-on.

When we reached the desk at the end of the hallway, there was an elderly police officer reading the newspaper. When he saw us, he folded it and asked, "What can I do for you?"

Samantha spoke up first. "We're here to make a statement," she said clearly, her voice steady despite her fear. "Officer Hellman told us to come in."

The police officer nodded and gestured for us to take a seat in front of him. "My name is Officer Clinton. A detective will take your statement. I'll let them know you are waiting."

The four of us sat down on scratched plastic chairs. Julianna and Charlotte pulled out their phones, while Samantha leaned into me and whispered, "Are you okay?"

"No," I sighed. My right leg was jumping up and down, so I placed a hand on it. "This is freaking me out. We're supposed to be enjoying a few days off together, and I didn't once imagine we'd be spending it in a police station. By the way, what did you want to talk to me about?"

I watched as Samantha's face paled. "It's important, but I'd rather do it somewhere private," she said firmly. Though her voice didn't shake, I could tell that something was wrong.

At that moment, a man wearing a ruffled gray suit that had seen better days walked through the door. He introduced himself as Detective Jones and shook all our hands before looking at Charlotte with a knowing look.

"Hope you've been doing alright since we sent Bart Holstein to prison," he winked.

Charlotte nodded in response and looked away, but her body language suggested that she was still uneasy about the situation. I glanced around the room; everyone seemed tense and uncomfortable except for the detective, who seemed to take it in his stride.

"Come with me to my office." Detective Jones ordered us, and the four of us followed him down another dreary beige hallway.

My heart was pounding so hard I thought it might burst

out of my chest. Every step felt like I was walking further and further away from the safety of the outside world. I wanted to turn around and run, but my feet kept moving forward.

We reached the detective's office, and he opened the door for us. Inside, there were four chairs lined up in front of a scratched metal desk. The room was small and cramped, with only a tiny window letting in a little light from the street outside. He gestured for us to sit down before taking his position on the edge of his desk.

The detective cleared his throat. "I'm aware of what happened at your office, Ms. Adams. But I hate to tell you this. We have no solid evidence placing Jody Agnew at the scene of any crime."

Charlotte punched her thigh. "We know it was her."

"The security footage shows a person with a ski mask on, and there is no forensic evidence supporting the theory that it was Ms. Agnew." Detective Jones shook his head back and forth. "But that doesn't mean it wasn't her. We know what type of person Jody Agnew is, and the company she keeps. I took the liberty of contacting the Federal Correctional Complex in Victorville, where Bart Holstein is serving out his sentence. According to the visitor's log, Jody Agnew has been there several times. Obviously, we don't know what they said to each other, but it does add more circumstantial evidence to the pile."

"But that doesn't help us," Charlotte muttered. "That man and his attack dog, Jody, are harassing me and my employees. It's got to stop."

I sat back in my chair, feeling dizzy from all the information being thrown at me. My hands were clammy with sweat as I tried to make sense of it all. Suddenly, Detective Jones leaned forward and locked eyes with me.

"Morgan," he said gently, "it's time for you to tell your version of the story."

My heart skipped a beat. Taking a deep breath, I recounted events as best as I could remember them. I tried to be as detailed as possible without speaking too quickly or getting myself lost in my words.

When I finished speaking, an uncomfortable silence hung in the air between us all.

"Ms. Bishop, is your version of events the same as Ms. Sterling's?" Detective Jones squinted his eyes at her.

"Yes sir," Samantha mumbled. "This situation is becoming unbearable. Please, keep us safe."

The door to his office opened, and an officer stuck his head in. "Detective Jones, may I speak to you for a moment?"

"Ladies," Detective Jones went to the door. "I'll be back in a few moments."

The four of us sat in silence, staring into our laps. Eventually, Charlotte cleared her throat and spoke up.

"We need to stick together," she said firmly. "If Julianna and I could get Bart Holstein off the streets, we can take care of Jody Agnew."

I glanced over at Charlotte in admiration. She was a strong woman who wasn't afraid to take on a challenge.

"Jody Agnew is nothing more than a bully," Charlotte continued. "She thinks she can outsmart everyone, but she's not infallible. We just need to be smart and stay one step ahead of her."

Julianna spoke up then. "Charlotte has a point," she

breathed. "Jody Agnew's weakness is her vanity; she believes she'll never be caught."

Samantha nodded her head in agreement while I felt my stomach sink; this was going to be much harder than I thought it would be.

"So you're telling me this woman has never been convicted of anything?" I glanced around in amazement. "We can do this," I said with determination in my voice.

The door to the office opened, and the detective came in and sat behind his desk.

"What's happening?" Julianna asked.

"Jody Agnew is being charged with misdemeanor vandalism for the damages she caused the thrift store." Detective Jones shook his head. "We have no evidence she did anything else."

I leapt to my feet. "This is insane! Don't you think it's a series of bizarre coincidences that this woman shows up at my hotel, then she breaks into ICE when I'm there signing the papers for my penthouse? And what about the Velvet Vixon, and now that stupid thrift store?" My temples throbbed. "Why can't the police do something?"

"Please, Ms Sterling." Detective Jones sighed. "She's now on our radar, and we'll..."

"For God's sake, Detective," Charlotte's voice now had an edge to it. "How much evidence do you need to put her away? We can't live our lives in fear."

"If we could convict her on circumstantial evidence, we would. But you don't have any proof that she's done anything wrong." The detective gestured for me to sit. "It's not a crime to go to the Chateau Marmont and try to speak to a movie star. She'll just tell the jury she's an over-excited fan. And the

Velvet Vixen?" Detective Jones shut his eyes. "She likes the ladies. Until we have her fingerprints, an eyewitness, or anything else that proves she's committed a crime, our hands are tied."

We sat silently for a moment, letting the news sink in.

"Then why did we even bother coming in?" Samantha snapped. "This is pointless."

"No, it's not." Detective Jones opened his eyes and smiled. "Now there's a paper trail. It's not much, but it's a start. I wish I had more positive new to tell you, but..." he waved his hands in the air and stood. "I have a meeting to attend. Here's my card." He handed all of us a business card. "Please contact me if anything else comes up."

My heart sank as we exited the detective's office. Nothing was going to be done about Jody Agnew—not yet, anyway. I glanced back at the door, wishing that Detective Jones could tell us he had figured out a way to arrest her.

But there was no such luck. We made our way through the lobby in a daze, each of us lost in our own thoughts about what this meant for us.

And then, I saw her—Jody Agnew. She was signing paperwork at the desk, a smug look on her face. She looked up when she noticed us and grinned as if she had won some kind of prize. With a flourish, she finished signing what she needed and sauntered out of the precinct like she owned the place.

My fists clenched as I watched her go. How could we ever be safe from her?

When we got outside, Jody was gone. Charlotte turned to us and spoke.

"It's going to be another week before the office is in good

enough condition for us to return. Work from home, and be careful. Never go out alone."

She and Julianna got into their car and left. Silently, Samantha and I got into her car.

"I have something very important to discuss with you," Samantha whispered. "I haven't been completely honest about something. Hopefully, you'll be able to forgive me."

Chapter Twenty-Three
Samantha

We drove the rest of the way to my apartment in silence. Anxiety and fear set in like a heavy fog. I didn't know what Morgan would think of me, or how she would react to my news. Dread and remorse filled my heart with an unbearable pressure, and my stomach was tied in knots. I'd done the best I could, but I felt like I was failing. I had to keep reminding myself that I made the right decision, given what I had known at the time. Still, I couldn't shake the guilt I felt for giving up my child for adoption all those years ago.

"Are you okay, Samantha?" Morgan laid her hand on mine. "Whatever it is, trust me, I'll be there for you."

I turned my head, and her vibrant eyes caught mine for a moment. "I'll tell you what's going on as soon as we're back at my place."

As we drove the few blocks to my apartment, all I could think about was how to tell Morgan the truth. My mind raced with a million thoughts and fears. I loved her so much, and I hoped she felt the same way. But could she ever forgive me for not telling her sooner? Would she stay with me after learning that I had given away a child all those years ago?

It was the first time in my life that I'd ever been truly in love, and I didn't want to lose it because of this dark part of my past. I wanted Morgan to understand why I did what I did, but how could she if she didn't even know the entire story?

The only thing that kept me going was the hope that one day she'd be able to accept me despite my past. With each passing moment, my resolve grew stronger. It was time to be honest and open up about who I really was - flaws and all.

We didn't speak for the rest of the drive. When we pulled into the parking lot of my building, Morgan laid her hand on my thigh and whispered, "Whatever it is, I'll be there for you."

A tear slid down my cheek, and Morgan reached over and wiped it away with her thumb.

I took a deep breath, and we got out of the car and entered the building. The elevator was thankfully empty. When we stepped out of it and made our way down the hall to my unit, my stomach was in knots. Morgan held my hand as we walked, her warm fingers entwined with mine. The silence between us felt heavy, almost like a burden.

When we reached my door, I turned to face her. She gave me a sad smile, understanding what I was feeling without me having to say anything. Then she leaned forward and kissed me softly on the lips.

"It's going to be okay," she whispered in my ear before pulling away from me and looking into my eyes again. "Whatever it is you have to tell me, I'm here for you."

I nodded and opened the door, gesturing for her to go first before following her inside. After laying my purse down, I faced her. "Would you mind giving me a few minutes before we talk? I have something important to do in my office."

"Sure," Morgan smiled. "Why don't I rustle us up something to eat? When you're ready to talk, I'll be here."

Morgan brushed her lips across mine, then kicked off her heels and padded into the kitchen. I toed my shoes off and walked into my home office and shut the door. After settling behind my desk, I pulled the envelope out that I'd received from the Mississippi Family Connection Bureau.

"I might not want to meet you, but I will tell you why. You deserve at least that much."

* * *

An hour later, I put my pen down, grabbed the letter I'd just written, and went to the kitchen. When I got there, I stood in the doorway for a moment, watching Morgan pull a casserole dish out of the oven.

"Whatever you made, it smells heavenly."

Morgan smiled. "It's *Mămăligă cu Brânză și Smântână,* polenta topped with cheese and sour cream. My grandmother used to make it for me. I hope you love it."

"Can we talk first?" I asked. After reading this letter, she might not want anything to do with me. "I have something to share with you."

"Of course." Morgan put the dish back in the oven. "This will stay warm while we talk."

She followed me to the living room, and I gestured for her to sit on the couch. I paced in front of her, hoping to find the right words.

"Samantha, just spit it out." Morgan's brow furrowed. "I'm a big girl, and I can handle whatever it is."

I took a deep breath and handed her the letter I'd written to the child I'd given up. "Before you read it, let me give you some context."

"Okay."

"Remember that envelope I took from you?" I asked and realized my voice was trembling. "It was from the Mississippi Family Connection Bureau. The reason I disappeared from Teeterville was because my parents sent me to a home for unwed mothers."

Morgan's mouth dropped open.

"I gave the child up for adoption, and now my biological son wants to reconnect with me." I felt pressure building behind my eyes. Please, Morgan, understand the decision I've made. "Here's a letter I've written him. Read it, and then we'll talk."

* * *

Hello.

I hope this letter finds you in good health and happiness. I've found myself struggling to put into words the emotions that have been with me for so long. My name is Samantha, and I am your birth mother.

Firstly, I want you to know that this letter comes from a place of sincerity and deep consideration. It's not easy for me to express what I feel, but I believe honesty is a fundamental aspect of any relationship, even one as complex as ours.

When I was a teenager, I faced a profound and overwhelming situation that changed the course of many lives, including yours. I made the heart-wrenching decision to place you for adoption. At that time, I was young and unable to provide the care and stability I believed a child deserved. Also, I didn't have a relationship any longer with your birth father, or with my parents. I haven't spoken with any of them since you were born, and you deserve a better family than the one I came from.

Over the years, I have thought about you often, wondering about the person you've become, the life you're living, and the family who I hope lovingly raised you. I pray that you were raised by people who love and respect you, and I sincerely hope you had a wonderful life filled with love and joy.

I need to express a hard truth. As much as I wish you the best, I don't feel emotionally capable of establishing a relationship with you. This decision is not a reflection of you or your worth; it's about my own limitations and the circumstances of our shared past.

I want to emphasize that this choice is not a rejection of you as an individual. You are not to blame for the decisions I made as a teenager. I am genuinely sorry if my decision brings any sadness or confusion.

My hope is that you understand that this choice is about my own emotional capacity and not a lack of care or concern for your well-being. I wish you a life filled with love, happiness, and all the success you deserve.

With sincere respect and warm wishes,

Samantha

Morgan and I sat in the dimly lit living room, the weight of our conversation lingering in the air. Her hand gently found mine, offering a silent reassurance as tears welled up in my eyes. The vulnerability in sharing the truth was overwhelming, and for a moment, neither of us spoke.

"I never expected... I never expected it to be this hard," I finally admitted, my voice barely above a whisper. Emotions that I'd bottled up for so long were now pouring out, and Morgan pulled me into an embrace.

"It's okay to feel all of this. You've been carrying it for so long," she whispered, her voice filled with compassion. Her arms wrapped around me, and I softly sobbed.

After a while, I pulled away, wiping away my tears. "I

never knew how much I needed to say those words until now," I confessed, managing a small, grateful smile.

"You've been so strong for so long. It's okay to let it out now," she reassured me, brushing away a stray tear from my cheek.

"Thank you, Morgan," I whispered

"Samantha, there's something..." She hesitated, and her gaze held mine. "I'm in love with you. And the fact that you shared something so deep and personal with me makes my love for you even stronger."

"I thought you'd want nothing to do with me," I sobbed, and Morgan took me in her arms again. "I told you Billy raped me, and then I just couldn't..."

"It's okay, baby." Morgan murmured. "You've been so strong for so long, with no one to help carry this burden. I mean it, Samantha. I love all of you."

For a moment, time seemed to freeze. Her words hung in the air, and I met her gaze, my heart pounding.

"I love you too, Morgan." I wiped the tears off my face with the palms of my hands. "The thought of losing you again, the way I lost you all those years ago, terrified me. My biological son attempted to contact me for the first time a few months ago. At the time, I tore up the letter and threw it away. I never expected him to try again. Then I went on a drinking binge, trying to forget the past."

"I probably would've done the same thing." Morgan stroked my hair, the feel of her fingers on my scalp sending shivers up and down my spine.

"I did everything I could to block out those memories. Then you arrived on the scene at the same time the second letter arrived from the bureau. My biggest fear was you'd think

I was a monster for not wanting to have a relationship with my, you know, son." I looked up at the ceiling and took a deep breath. "But I can't. My son wasn't conceived out of love, and I never want him to know what happened. Plus, I'm tired of reliving the past. What I want is a future, and I'm hoping and praying you'll want to spend that future with me." I took her hand, then stared into her eyes. "I love you Morgan."

I leaned in, closing my eyes as I inched closer. My heart raced and my lips trembled before they made contact with hers. As our mouths moved together, I felt warmth radiating through me. All anxiety melted away and in its place was a feeling of calm.

Breaking apart from her, I looked up into her eyes, my heart full of love. She smiled back at me; her gaze never wavering. "I'll always be here for you," Morgan murmured, taking my hand in hers. "No matter what."

"And I'll always be there for you, my love."

Epilogue
Morgan- 18 Months Later

"Darling, we don't want to be late," I called out to Samantha. "The beauty team is expecting us in an hour. Oh, and the hairdresser is meeting us at Monolo's studio."

"I swear to God I feel like I'm going to throw up," Samantha called from the bathroom. "Aren't you even the slightest bit nervous? It's not every day you're nominated for an Oscar."

"It's okay, darling," I said soothingly as I stepped into the bathroom. "It's natural to be nervous, but you'll be fine once we get there." I wrapped my arms around her and gave her a tight hug. "You look stunning."

Of course, I was a bundle of nerves, but the thrill of being nominated was more important to me than winning. It's highly unlikely I'll win, considering both Jennifer and Emma are my competition.

As I touched up my face with moisturizer, I couldn't help but feel a combination of excitement and anxiety. Even after all these years in the business, attending the Academy Awards still felt like a huge honor for me. I knew I would be mingling with famous actors, directors, and producers who have achieved great success.

At this point in my journey as an actress, attending the Academy Awards was a dream come true. This wasn't my first time at a high-profile awards show. I'd already been nominated and lost at the Golden Globes, but the Academy Awards were different. More prestigious, and though I doubted I'd win best actress, if I do it would mean a lot more money and roles.

"You're going to be great," Samantha said, her voice full of affection and admiration. "No matter what happens at the ceremony, I'm so proud of you." She gave me a tight hug and kissed me on the forehead. "Win or lose, you're still my winner in my book," she added with a smile.

I took a deep breath and let it out slowly as I looked at myself in the mirror again.

Despite the overwhelming emotions running through me, I was also excited to get dressed up for the night. The designer Monolo Velázquez loaned us two stunning gowns—one for each of us—and hair and makeup artists were meeting us at his studio later that day. All I could think about was how amazing it would feel to slip into those gorgeous dresses. The only part I hated was getting my hair and makeup done. I always felt like they used too much war paint, and I swear hairdressers were closet sadists.

Samantha put her arm around me, and we stared at our reflection in the mirror. "Right now, we look like we just got home from the gym," she smirked. We were both in sweats, sneakers, and had no makeup on. "But in a few hours, you, my darling, will be the most stunning woman in the universe."

* * *

I stood in the middle of the studio, in awe of my reflection. I was wearing a beautiful blue gown with intricate detailing and an elegant silhouette. Monolo made the dress of layered tulle and lace that cascaded down to the ground, giving the dress an ethereal feel. The bodice was beaded with sparkling sequins and crystals, creating a stunning effect as it caught the light. The neckline was low cut and accented by an off-the-shoulder drape of fabric that trailed around my arms.

My hair had been pulled back into an elaborate updo, and my makeup had been done expertly to accentuate my features while still keeping it subtle. I felt like a different person—someone glamorous and poised for the red carpet.

But while I looked amazing on the outside, I couldn't help but feel out of place. Even after years as an actress, these glossy events still felt a bit foreign to me—I was so much more comfortable in jeans and t-shirts than in couture gowns and designer shoes. It would take some getting used to if I wanted to make it through this night with grace—but at least I looked good in the meantime.

"Oh my stars, you're gorgeous," Samantha said when she walked in. She kissed my exposed shoulder. "Monolo has outdone himself."

"You, my dear, look like a Disney princess come to life," I grinned. She was wearing a breathtaking copper-colored gown that shimmered and shone with every step she took. The fabric hugged her curves perfectly, and the intricate beading along the bodice was stunning. Her hair had been crafted into an elaborate up-do with delicate tendrils framing her face, and her makeup was immaculate—highlighting her natural beauty without overdoing it.

Samantha looked like a million bucks, and I could see the excitement on her face. She may have been nervous, but there was no mistaking the determination in her eyes. Ever since we reunited, her real estate business had flourished. I knew she was happy to support me at the Academy Awards, but this was also a business opportunity for her. Now that we were together and hobnobbing with celebrities, they wanted to buy property from her. The public might think that I'm the star, but Samantha actually made more money than I did, and I was hardly poor.

"Ladies, you look marvelous!" Monolo circled around us, making minor adjustments to our gowns, as he did. "Now remember, when those stupid fashionistas ask where you got your lovely gowns, pronounce my name slowly so they remember it." He backed away a few feet, his gaze like a laser beam. "You're going to win, Morgan. I can feel it in my bones!"

* * *

My heart raced as we stepped out onto the red carpet. There was a throng of people—reporters, photographers, fans—all clamoring to get a glimpse of me. I squinted in the bright lights and tried to keep my smile firmly in place as I posed for photos with Samantha at my side.

"Who made your dress?" A reporter shouted, then two more asked the same thing.

"Monolo Velázquez." I replied, then slowly spun around. "Our gowns were custom made for us."

"You know, I could get used to this," Samantha whispered through a smile. She loved the big events more than I did.

Samantha and I made our way down the red carpet, waves of cheers washing over us like a tide. Everywhere I looked, there were people craning their necks for a better view or screaming my name.

"This is surreal," I whispered to her, and Samantha took my hand and squeezed it.

"You deserve it, darling."

We paused in front of the giant doors of the Dolby Theatre while security double-checked our names on the list. Then we took a deep breath and stepped inside.

Inside, everything was calm compared to outside—no flashing cameras or screaming fans here—just rows and rows of empty seats waiting patiently for their occupants. The ceiling soared high above us in an intricate pattern of golds and blues that resembled an ornate tapestry crafted by hand centuries ago.

"This looks so different from the way it does on television," Samantha murmured. "Damn it, I wish we'd come a little later. No one is here yet."

"Trust me, we came at the best time. No rushing, and the cameras stayed on us instead of rushing to the next celebrity. Come on, let's sit before Eva and Billy arrive."

* * *

"You've got this, Morgan," Eva rubbed my shoulder. She was being an exceptionally good sport, considering she'd lost the Oscar for best director.

"You're our last hope for a win," Billy said. "I've won a

Tony, so I know what it's like to win. I might have lost out this time to Brad, but I know deep in my bones you've got this."

Billy was putting on a cheery face, considering his run of bad luck recently. After filming on *Echoes of Elysium* concluded, his wife left him. Drugs were the culprit, and after six weeks at a treatment facility in Palm Springs, he looked much better.

Chris Evans, one of Hollywood's biggest stars, strolled onto the stage and a hush fell. He grinned at the audience, waved his hand in greeting, then opened the envelope and read out the nominees.

"For best actress," he declared, "we have Jennifer Lawrence for *Red Rover*." A video montage played on the screen over Chris's head. Jennifer looked stunning in a red Balenciaga gown.

"Emma Watson for *The Imitation Game*." He grinned, and the camera panned to Emma, who was looking a little green.

"You've got this darling, I swear." Samantha squeezed my hand. A woman strolled across the stage and handed Chris the envelope.

"And Morgan Sterling for *Echoes of Elysium!*" He paused dramatically before continuing, "and this year's Oscar goes to... Morgan Sterling!"

I screamed into my hands, then tried to stand up, but my legs were shaking. Finally, I got to my feet and walked down the aisle

I rushed up onto the stage and hugged Chris Evans as he handed me the golden statue.

When I looked out into the crowd, I saw Samantha jumping up and down with tears streaming down her face; Eva was standing next to her with a proud smile; and Billy was clapping with them. Words couldn't express how much their support meant to me at that moment.

I took hold of the microphone and cleared my throat before speaking. "I'm truly amazed by this honor," I said, looking around at all those smiling faces. "This isn't just a win for me—it's a win for every woman who has ever pursued her dream in spite of all odds."

"I know I only have a few moments, but I need to thank Eva Thorne. She is one helluva director, and Billy, I love you to pieces. But most of all, I need to thank my wife, Samantha. She was there for all my little breakdowns during filming, boosting my spirits when I struggled. Samantha," the camera panned down to our table. She was dabbing at her eyes with an embroidered handkerchief. "I love you more than anything. Without you, I'm nothing."

Thank you for reading Morgan and Samantha's love story. It was truly a wonderful experience writing it.

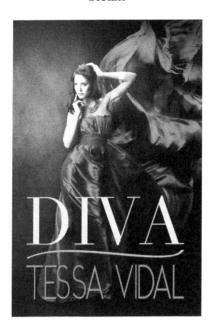

The following is an excerpt of the novel Diva, the story of an opera singer who falls in love with her personal assistant.

* * *

I woke up face down on the couch, my phone buzzing on the coffee table in front of me. I turned over and yawned, the last wisps of a dream I couldn't recall evaporating away. Someone had sent me a text, and my heart skipped a beat when I realized it might be Maria. When I saw who the message was from, I nearly flung the phone across the room.

My ex-girlfriend, Marilyn.

Since it was a little after nine Saturday morning, I was reasonably sure she wasn't drunk texting. We'd broken up three years ago, and about every six months she'd call or text while bombed out of her mind. It was always the same thing.

She missed me, wished things had gone differently, and would I be interested in hanging out sometime soon?

The first few times I went along with it, swept up in a tide of nostalgia. Gone were the bad times, the drunken arguments and the constant feeling of unease. Then, after *hanging out,* Marilyn would show her true colors. She knew every insecurity of mine and played them like an out of tune piano, jangly notes that made me cringe.

"Hell no. I'm not replying to that." I grumbled and laid the phone down on the table. It buzzed again. "Marilyn, you're working my last good gay nerve." I stood,walked into the bathroom, and took a long hard look at myself in the mirror. Finally, for the first time in three years, I was truly over her. The angst and despair I used to feel whenever she'd text or call was absent, replaced by irritation and a sad sense of loss.

"I loved you once, Marilyn, I really did. But, it's time for you to move on. I have." I murmured, then walked back into the living room to see what she wanted. There were three texts. The first two were from my ex, while the third one was from Maria.

> Sorry

> I know it's your day off, but I need a few things and don't know where to find them

> Rooibos Tea

> Cough Syrup

> Vicks VapoRub

> Sugar Free Vitamin C lozenges

> If you could get them for me I'll make it up to you soon

Steam

> I swear I'll leave you alone for the rest of the weekend

That didn't sound good. I texted Maria back.

> Are U sick?

A minute passed, and I wondered if she'd changed her mind. Finally, she replied.

> Yes

I tossed the phone on to the couch, ran into the bathroom and turned on the hot water in the shower. It was an old building, and the water took a couple of minutes to warm up. Then I raced into the living room and sent her a text back.

> Jumping into the shower now
>
> Be there asap

* * *

An hour and a half later I showed up at Maria's apartment with bags of medicines, teas and my secret cold and flu medicine; Mom's chicken soup.

After two weeks of working for her, we'd grown comfortable enough for me to just let myself in. When I opened her door, it was like walking into a hot humid jungle, minus the plants and creepy critters. By now, all nine of the humidifiers I'd ordered for Maria had arrived, and she must have had each one running at full blast. I put the bags down in the kitchen, found a stock pot and began warming up the chicken soup I'd had frozen in my freezer.

"What are you doing?"

Maria was standing in the kitchen doorway wearing her customary skin-hugging t-shirt and pink sweatpants. Her tan arms glistened in the humid air. I forced my eyes up to face level and replied, "I have a secret weapon against colds, flus, and any other pesky crap you can think of. My mom's chicken soup."

"You don't have to do all this. I gave you the weekend off and..."

I held my hand up. "Stop. It's no problem at all. Oh, and I got you the stuff you wanted." I detected a hint of congestion in her voice, and Maria's eyes were bloodshot. "What the hell is rooibos tea, anyway?"

Maria grinned, and I noticed the darkness under her eyes. She looked like she hadn't slept. "It's an herbal tea from South Africa, also known as red bush tea. Rooibos is loaded with antioxidants and other stuff my voice teacher claimed would cure anything."

"I'll heat up some water for you." I reached into the cabinet next to the stove and pulled out the kettle.

"So, does your mother live close by? How did she make this soup so fast?" Maria asked, yawning at the same time. I glanced up to see her stretching her arms over her head, pulling the too-tight t-shirt up and exposing her flat stomach.

"I made it from her recipe. Mom lives in Youngstown, Ohio." I turned on the burner, then opened the box of tea. "When I was a kid, she'd make this whenever we were sick, and I swear by it. Didn't your mom have a special thing she'd do for you when you were ill?"

"The same as your mother. *Sopa de Pollo* and Vicks VapoRub were her remedies." Maria replied, surprising me.

"I thought you were German, or Swiss?" I asked. Marilyn was Mexican-American, and I recognized the Spanish name of chicken soup.

"I am. My mother is from Puerto Rico, and my father was from Berlin. He died when I was young, so Mom moved to Connecticut where her family had relocated. She's an amazing cook, but we're not very..." Maria said. But then the kettle whistled. She crossed the room before I could react, reached around me and grabbed it off the burner. Her lavender scent permeated the air, and it took considerable self-control not to grab her t-shirt and inhale it from the source. Instead, I decided to get the object of my lust into another room so I could focus on the food.

"Go watch TV or something. I'll take care of your lunch."

"Seriously, Caroline, you don't have to..." Maria started, but I cut her off.

"I have no other plans, plus you have a big week coming up. If you're not healthy, that means I'm not working. So let me do my job, which is making sure you are happy, healthy and ready to perform." What I didn't add was that if I wasn't here, I'd be sitting at home thinking about her, with the help of my vibrator and porn.

"You're the boss." Maria grinned, throwing her hands up in the air in mock surrender. She placed a teabag in her mug of water and left the kitchen.

* * *

"Here you go." I placed a tray on the coffee table in front of her with *two* bowls of soup. If I was going to be here cooking for Maria, she'd have to put up with me eating with her. We didn't spend much time doing non-work related things. Our days were filled with rehearsals, social media, and me running errands. Aside from the fact that she was a somewhat famous singer who was neurotic about her voice, I knew very little about what made Maria tick.

"This is amazing." Maria murmured after the first spoonful. "Thank you."

I started in on my bowl, occasionally sneaking glances at Maria. She had a blanket covering her lap, holding the warm bowl in one hand and the spoon in another. With each spoonful, she seemed to appreciate the flavors, allowing the comforting warmth to envelop her senses. Of course that was my imagination. Who knows how she really felt about the damned soup, but my brain went into overdrive whenever I was around Maria.

"So, what do you do for fun?" I asked after she'd finished her bowl. Maria turned away from me, snatched a tissue out of a box next to her, and wiped her nose. Even with a cold, she was still stunning. "Besides turning your apartment into the biggest sauna in Raleigh."

Maria rolled her eyes and laughed, which turned into a tiny cough. "Well, the reason for the sauna is that I can't afford to get sick, and the heat and humidity is best for my throat. That's why I'm always drinking warm water."

"I figured that about the water. So, aside from singing, what do you like to do?" I hoped I wasn't overstepping a boundary, but I wanted to know what made Maria tick. You know, so I could either find a reason not to be attracted, or so I could add another layer to my hopeless fantasy about her.

Maria paused, staring straight ahead at the blank television screen on the opposite wall. "Well, I read mostly. Sometimes I play online backgammon. But, my career is my thing. I don't have a lot of time for much else."

For a split second, I felt pity. Here she was, one of the most beautiful women I'd ever seen, who had a career most people would envy, and she literally had no life outside of her work.

"You need to go out more, because it sounds like you live in a retirement village or something." *Shit.* That didn't come out right. "I'm sorry. I shouldn't have said that." I mumbled, my cheeks burning. In the blurry reflection on the flat screen TV I noticed Maria's shoulders stiffen, and then she sighed.

"I've spent many years working, and as you are learning, it isn't an easy job. When I lost my voice..." Maria's tone grew somber, "I thought I'd lost everything. Singing is everything to me, and if that means not having much of a life?" She shrugged then pulled another tissue out of the box.

"Hey, do you remember that list you gave me on my first day?" I asked. Maria nodded. "At the very bottom you asked me where a good karaoke bar was. As soon as you're better, I'm taking you to Flex. Every Sunday night they have *scaryoke*, which is filled with non-singers like me singing off key. It's fun." As soon as the words popped out of my mouth, I regretted it. Flex was a gay bar, mostly for men, and I was still clueless about which team Maria played on.

Maria laughed. "I love karaoke. It's fun to sing stuff non-opera related. Maybe after the performances are done next week, we can go." Then she grabbed the remote and switched on the television. "This is the first time I've turned it on since I moved in. I usually watch documentaries, but I bet that's not your thing. Am I right?"

I swiveled my head to answer, and she was lightly biting down on her lower lip. I nodded, though I would've watched anything Maria wanted just so I could sit next to her for a while longer.

"What do you want to watch?" Maria navigated to the guide channel, and I felt her shoulder press against mine.

Well, I guessed that meant she wanted me to hang out. My heart thumped in my chest. "When I'm feeling crappy, I watch eighties movies. I don't know why, but they always make me feel better."

"Okay." Maria said as the TV listings ran down the screen. Then I saw the one movie I *didn't* want to see. The film that virtually guaranteed that my inappropriate fantasies about my boss would become even more pathetic and desperate.

"Oh, that's a good one, and it's from the eighties too." Maria clicked the remote. And of course, it was *that* movie, the one that always made me cry. I snuck a glance at her and noticed Maria's broad smile. She really wanted to watch it.

"*Fuck.*" I muttered under my breath, then hoped she hadn't heard.

"Excuse me?" Maria lifted an eyebrow. "Did you want to watch something else?"

"No no, I love *Moonstruck*. It's one of my favorite films of all time."

* * *

"That movie gets to you, huh?" Maria asked, looking down at the crumpled kleenex in my hand. I nodded, and she switched off the TV. "Me too."

I couldn't tell if she'd cried or not since her eyes were already red from her cold. A cold I might catch since I'd been breathing in her air for the last two hours while her shoulder stayed glued to mine. But I didn't care. Maria could have had Ebola and I still would've watched Cher and Nicolas Cage fall in love onscreen by her side. We sat there for a few more moments until the silence and tension-filled air became too much for me to bear. I rose to my feet.

"Let me head on out. There's more soup on the stove in case you're hungry. Do you need anything else?" I asked, hoping she'd ask me to stay, but afraid that she would, too.

Maria shook her head no, then stood up and walked me to the door.

"Thanks." Maria murmured. "I'm glad you were here with me. I get a little... too much in my own head sometimes." Her voice caught at the end of her sentence, and when I met Maria's gaze, there was a heat I'd never seen before, though it was probably because she was sick. She opened the door and stood back to let me walk by.

"Anytime." I murmured. "See you Tuesday."

I stood in front of the elevator and pressed the down button, then spun around. "You know, if you..." I began, but the door was already shut.

About the Author

Tessa Vidal is a feel young woman in her fifties. By day she's a church secretary, but at night, she writes tales of love between woman that stand the test of time.

Also by Tessa Vidal

Crave

The Promise

Reunited

A Second Chance

Passion

Diva

ICE

Milton Keynes UK
Ingram Content Group UK Ltd.
UKHW020246221123
432980UK00016B/941

9 798223 696841